WRAP AND TURN

Tink Tank Knitting Mystery #1

JESSA ARCHER

Archer Mysteries

Wrap and Turn

Charlotte "Charlie" Shaw is a divorcée and empty nester running a knitting store/coffee shop in a rural Iowa college town. Her biggest problem is the guy who runs the tattoo parlor next door, Mike Blankenship, letting his customers run amok, playing death metal at two a.m., littering, and vandalizing the neighborhood.

When that cad turns up as a cadaver, Charlie becomes a suspect. The more Charlie unravels the killer's web, the more she realizes that she and her employees are targets too. Will she unmask the killer before she and her close-knit community become the next victims?

Chapter One

HARVEY and I blew in the back door with a rush of frigid air and a few ephemeral snowflakes. I unhooked his leash and let him go. We'd just completed our predawn neighborhood walk and returned to home base, a downtown building in Abingdon, Iowa, where we live and work.

Harvey padded out before me as I ambled into the store, inhaling the earthy scent of freshly ground coffee, with a sharp waft of a dark roast brewing, the underlying sweetness of syrups and pastries, and the clean, fresh scent of dyed yarn. These are the aromas of the Tink Tank, the best accomplishment of my life (aside from my two grown sons), a knitting store with a coffee shop tucked in front.

The coffee brings lots of people in, but the comfy seating and the lively atmosphere make them linger. Knitters come in, not just to peruse the stock, but also to meet with friends and hold club meetings, to take classes, or to simply sit and relax with their projects and a nice beverage.

The Tink Tank is one of many gems in the downtown section of this small city with its tree-lined streets and historic buildings filled with interesting little shops, all nestled close to

Eastern Iowa University. College students, professors, people who work downtown, even people driving over from other parts of the city and in from the outlying county are all familiar faces every day.

As I hung up Harvey's leash, I saw Gina had made it down before me today, which made me feel guilty. I was moving a little slower than usual. It had been a rough week and it wasn't over yet. I was praying that the mess with my shop's webstore would resolve very, very soon.

I was definitely in need of a big dose of java. The *real* kind, not that website nonsense.

"Time for morning ear wubbies!" Gina came around the counter, her bobbed dark hair swinging around her face, and crouched down to Harvey's level, offering him his first treat of the day.

Whereas I lean toward ease in my personal style—no makeup, jeans, and a comfy blouse, prematurely white hair braided down my back—Gina is more edgy in the way that only young people can pull off.

She wears what I'd call a sort of pastel-Goth style—pale face, dark lipstick, dark eye makeup, and chunky black boots. To mostly black garments she adds soft pastel accents for contrast. Her casual tees, primarily ordered from Japan, tend to feature cute creatures like cats or pandas accompanied by dreadfully dark text, knives, or something equally depressing. Odd juxtapositions. She thinks it's hilarious and it suits her personality. No matter what she wears, she's stinkin' adorable, and since we all wear aprons in the store, the more staid Midwesterners among my clientele aren't bothered.

Harvey's tail loudly slapped a chair behind him and his whole body wriggled as he crunched through his treats and then snuffled her hands to see if she had any more. I loved watching Gina and Harvey together. She was his "mama from another llama," or so I joked.

Gina gave Harvey a second treat and stroked his ears enthusiastically—the aforementioned "wubbies." They finished their daily ritual with Harvey giving her a paw before he sauntered off to his bed in my tiny office at the back of the store. He would spend most of the day there unless he heard a favorite customer's voice and I gave him the okay signal.

Gina shot me a knowing look. "Someone had a bath last night."

"Once a week, every week," I said through a smile that was a little forced.

I pulled a double shot of espresso for myself and downed it, hoping it would kick in fast. The last few days had been exhausting, and I'd had to force myself to put Harvey through his bathing routine the night before.

He had been a good boy, as always, with his tongue hanging out in a big panting smile while I soaped, rinsed, conditioned, rinsed, combed, dried, and brushed him until my arms ached and there were no more loose hairs flying up my nose.

Harvey is a gentle giant. Everyone in town loves him and he knows it. I truly believe that in his mind he exists to be loved by everyone he meets. But he's also a Great Pyrenees, weighing in at a whopping 116 pounds at his last vet visit. And the fur on that boy—oh, so much fur. He was in the final stages of blowing his coat for the spring, so I had to be extra vigilant about maintaining it. That meant daily brushing and extra cleaning in the shop. No one wants to find a snow-white hair floating in their latte.

I try to maintain a schedule of bathing him every Sunday night without fail, since Sunday is our early day to close with no scheduled evening activities, but I hadn't managed it that week. I'd been too busy frantically trying to fix my website headaches. As I'd swept up the night before, however, a few white tumbleweeds at the rear of the shop had made a thorough grooming an immediate imperative. I couldn't put it off another day no matter what my creaky fifty-three-year-old bones had to say about it.

After the bath I'd collapsed in bed, foregoing dinner or even a snack. I slept so hard I didn't even notice whether the store next door had been up to its usual shenanigans late into the night. A small mercy.

I dismissed that thought and threw a clean apron over my head. There was a lot to do to get everything back on track, and I was determined that today was going to be better than the last few. The sun was about to make its appearance over Abingdon, Iowa, and I was going to make it a great day, do everything on my to-do list, and smile through it all, even if it hurt.

Gina straightened and went to wash up before returning to our morning duties, like filling the burr-grinder hoppers and brewing up batches of our signature blends.

I unlocked the door, flipped the sign to open, and moved behind the counter to join her. There was a lot to do before the morning rush.

I smacked my lips, my tongue still coated with the bitter residue of the espresso. I searched my pockets and found a small roll of breath mints. "Mint?" I offered Gina. "My breath is kickin'."

Gina glanced at me with a dubious smile.

"What? Didn't I use that word right?"

She giggled. "Oh, no. You did. You're progressing nicely." Then she held up her index and middle fingers in front of her mouth and made a kicking motion. "Yup."

I laughed.

It's not like I'm trying to fit in with all the young people I work with and serve, I just don't want to be an artifact—so the many college students who come in feel at home. I want them to feel free to linger for hours to study, work, or meet other students. I want to build community.

So, I try out some of the phrases I've picked up on Gina before letting them loose as a part of my general vocabulary. She's young enough to serve as a bridge across the generational gap and honest enough to tell me when I'm making a fool of myself.

Gina had been a godsend for me and for the store. Within months of hiring her, she'd made herself indispensable. She knows knitting, she knows coffee, and she has enough energy for three people. The customers enjoy her cheerful demeanor, and she's willing to work hours that fit in around everyone else's odd schedules, working on her Ph.D. research when she's not needed in the store. I'd promoted her to assistant manager and hadn't regretted it for a second. She'd become my tenant and neighbor in the other apartment above the shop. And she was a very dear friend.

I dread the day she'll finish her dissertation. Once she graduates, she'll move on, move *away*, just like my sons did. While I'm sure I'll find a competent assistant to replace her when the time comes, losing that close friendship will be devastating.

I was distracted from that depressing thought when Vincent popped his head in a few minutes later, delivering pastries and chocolates from his patisserie down the street called Ganache. Vincent is slightly built, about my age, with plain spectacles and thinning hair that he only recently stopped combing over. Wearing a pristine white apron over his conservative blue shirt and tie, he set the large white boxes on the counter with a soft sigh. "Another mess in the alley this morning," he said.

My brows drew together in confusion as I started filling the glass display case with his tempting treats. "I didn't see anything when Harvey and I went for our walk."

"There were some broken bottles, so I cleaned it up as soon as I saw it—I didn't want you or Harvey to get hurt in the dark."

Ugh. Broken bottles where all the owners and tenants parked their cars and delivery drivers pulled up. I hoped Vincent had gotten it all in the meager light of the safety lamp out back so no one turned up with a flat.

"That's awfully nice of you, Vincent. I wish that hadn't been necessary." I immediately switched gears to foam some milk and pull a shot of espresso for Vincent's favorite drink.

Trance, the tattoo parlor next door, had a habit of letting their clientele go a bit wild into the wee hours, playing loud music and leaving rubbish behind—usually empty beer cans, snack wrappers, and cigarette butts—both in the alley and on the street out front. Sometimes worse—sometimes they vandalized the neighborhood.

Ninety-nine times out of one hundred Vincent or I cleaned up after them instead of Mike Blankenship, the shop's owner, which was an ongoing source of stress for every business on this side of the block. Mainly the two of us, though, since our shops flanked his.

Harvey poked his head out of the office, his snow-white pom-pom of a tail gently swaying over his back.

"Hey, there's the big man!" Vincent said, his manner changing completely.

Everyone is like that with Harvey. His joyful smiling expression always seem to have a positive impact on someone's mood, no matter how sour. I'd been told again and again by my sister that animals and business didn't mix. In this special case, she was dead wrong, and I was so glad I didn't make Harvey stay shut up in my apartment on the third floor all day every day.

"Okay, Harvey," I called.

Harvey sauntered out and accepted daily treat number

three from Vincent, along with a moment of requisite petting, before retiring again to his bed.

I handed Vincent his coffee with an extra pump of Tahitian vanilla. Vincent liked his drinks extra sweet. I couldn't fathom how he stayed so thin, given what he did for a living. I'd be far rounder if I had to control myself around those temptations all day. "My way of saying thanks."

Vincent grinned. He took a step toward the door. "I won't say no to that. How's the website snafu coming?"

I purged the steam wand and wiped it down. "Cameron at Comp Time helped us out. He got all the product codes back in order by using an older version of the site. He's still trying to track down how it happened. He thinks we were hacked."

My left eyelid started to twitch. Somehow all the product codes on my website had gotten mixed up. And when orders were filled by my part-time student employees over a three-to-four-day span, customers had been sent the wrong items. All the expensive product codes had been swapped for cheaper ones. For example, someone who ordered cashmere yarn got acrylic instead. Another person purchased rosewood crochet hooks and received plastic ones. Someone else asked for one-hundred-gram balls of superwash merino sock yarn and was sent twenty-five-gram balls of a glitzy eyelash yarn. It was an absolute nightmare.

At ten to twenty online orders per day, that was a lot of unhappy customers. We were doing our best to make up for it by sending free gifts and extras when we sent out their intended orders and not requiring them to send back the mistaken products. My site had also been down for days while I scrambled to figure out what had gone wrong. The debacle put a huge dent in my profit, and probably my reputation.

Over the last five years, I'd become relatively well-known as a specialty yarn and fiber merchant. I'd developed my own proprietary lines from fibers milled and sourced locally. My yarns were special and unique. None of that had been easy. It felt like all that effort had been trashed overnight.

And all this three weeks before the biggest event I would host this year. The timing couldn't be worse.

Vincent looked confused. "Hacked? Who would hack a knitting store?"

I shrugged helplessly. None of it made sense to me. I didn't know if I'd clicked some doomsday setting by accident and screwed everything up, or if my computer had malfunctioned, but it was looking more and more like I was an innocent party in this.

Vincent put his hand on the door, frowning. I saw Marilyn coming up the sidewalk outside—our first customer of the day, as usual. The shop's phone rang. I grabbed a pen and reached for the cordless as I waved goodbye to Vincent. "Tink Tank. This is Charlie Shaw."

"Charlie? This is Cameron at Comp Time. You have a minute? I thought I'd try to catch you super early. You can be hard to get ahold of."

I looked at Gina. She shooed me with her hands and kept working. I moved toward my office. "I have a few minutes before the morning rush starts. What's up?"

Gina had recommended that I go to Comp Time with this problem. Apparently Cameron was more than just a local repair guy—he was also what she called a talented white-hat hacker. He'd recently moved his business to Abingdon from Chicago to take care of his aging parents. I wasn't sure what a white-hat hacker was. Gina knew a lot more about these sorts of things. But he seemed to be a good guy who knew an awful lot about computers and Wi-Fi and all that. I trusted Gina on this one and so far, Cameron hadn't let me down.

"I have some answers for you. You're not going to like them."

I plopped down in my desk chair. Harvey opened his eyes

and rolled them over at me without moving. "Lay it on me, Cameron. I want to know what happened."

He drew in a noisy breath, like he was reluctant to keep talking. "I was right. It was a hack. I know you don't know all the technical terms, so I'll try to simplify. The person who did this didn't use any finesse. It was a blunt attack. They didn't try to hide their trail. It was pretty easy to track down their IP address."

My stomach flipped over and I felt some acid rising in my throat. I'd been working so hard all these years to make this shop a success. Finding out that someone actually wanted to do my business harm was nauseating.

"So you have their IP address? Is that like a mailing address for their computer?" I asked, my face heating up from my lack of knowledge on the topic. I don't like playing the part of the out-of-touch old lady. It smarts.

"It's a specific set of numbers assigned to every computer by their Internet service provider, and it's associated with the physical address where the computer connects to the internet. It can change if you reset your modem or use a laptop with someone else's Wi-Fi. But I don't think that's what happened in this case." He paused and sighed. "The computer that hacked yours is located at 527 Main Street."

I stood up. My desk chair slid back and slammed into the wall.

I knew that address too well.

The address of my store was 529 Main Street.

Mike Blankenship, the crapulent donkey patoot that owned Trance, had hacked my website.

"Are you still there, Charlie?"

I sagged back into my chair. "Is this provable? Like in a court of law?"

He made a funny sound, like flapping air through his lips. "You'd have to talk to a lawyer. But I bet it'd be expensive and

I doubt they could make you any guarantees. The Internet is kind of the Wild West still, to be honest. Are your losses that bad?"

"It's the principle of the thing. That guy—" I cut myself off before I said something unsavory. My sister preaches that a good businessperson never allows their professionalism to fall away. Ever.

"I've heard the stories. I'm glad my shop is a few blocks away. I'd love to be closer to campus, but... sheesh. Not if that's what I'd have to put up with for a neighbor."

Cameron talked me through my options to prevent anything like this from happening in the future—all things I should have done when I set up my online shop years before. Early on, it had been about money. I tried to do everything I could myself because I didn't know if I'd make it with the shop in general.

Later, it had become more about time. I was too busy to do everything I needed to. Things just fell off my to-do list and I forgot about them. Cameron assured me he could do all of it for me easily and quickly for minimal cost. We made an appointment and I circled it three times on my calendar in red sharpie.

When I got off the phone with him, I sat there stewing. What was I going to do about this? Should I confront Mike Blankenship? Should I just ignore it and put the protections in place so he couldn't do it again? Was that even enough? What else was he willing to do to mess with me? Should I get a restraining order or something?

Mike had rented the building next door for about as long as I'd owned mine, but his business had really taken off a few years ago. That was when the midnight death metal and garbage issues had come to a head.

In the beginning, I'd brought him coffee and pastries and

smiled as I asked him to please keep the noise to a minimum and encourage his customers to use a trash can.

But I didn't catch any flies with that honey. He'd smirked at me and nothing had changed. Then, about a month before, I'd heard some unsavory rumors about Mike mistreating women and I lost all interest in trying to be nice about the noise. I'd taken to calling the police department to report noise disturbances instead. I was losing sleep, and something had to give.

There were plenty of apartments above the shops on this street that had to be affected by the noise, but maybe I was the only one who had ever complained to his face. So he had just one individual to pin his anger on. And this was his retaliation for calling the police.

I desperately wanted to talk to someone about it, but I couldn't. Not yet. Not in the store. I'd have to wait to talk to Gina that evening.

I could call my sister…

I cringed. She'd be outraged that I'd let the website safeguards fall by the wayside and lecture me for days. She was always on me about "letting the pros handle things." And I knew she wasn't wrong in this case. I'd made a mistake.

Still, I was tempted to call her. Once she stopped scolding, she might have good suggestions for how I could deal with this. She had decades of experience working with the public.

My sons would want to help, but they had their own busy lives and would both be at work. Not to mention that they lived too far away to be more than a sympathetic ear. I wouldn't bother them with this.

Another thought occurred to me. I'd inquired with a real estate agent a few weeks before about the cost of buying the building next door—the very same building Mike Blankenship's Trance occupied.

I had just wanted to know if the owner would be willing to sell it to me if I opted to expand my shop. They had, and the price had been fair. But the building next door was really run down. The owner was elderly and hadn't maintained it properly for decades. It would need a ton of work to knock down the walls between the two adjacent buildings and bring the new space up to the same level as the Tink Tank.

Expanding the shop would give both the coffee side and the knitting side more room to breathe. It would allow me to have a bigger space for knitting classes. A lot more space for people to linger and talk, which was exactly what I wanted—a place for the community to gather.

At that time I'd been undecided about whether I wanted to invest all the money I'd saved up in expanding the shop or buying my first home since the divorce, so I could move out of the apartment on the third floor. I hadn't really been all that serious.

But now…

Now, I felt like the balance was swaying toward store expansion.

I picked up the phone again. My heart pounded in my throat. Would I do it? Would I start the financial proceedings that would upend my life, plunge the store into chaos for months, put me back in debt, and keep me in the apartment for who knew how long?

I hesitated. I shouldn't be impulsive. I should talk to the people who were my best advisors first.

And maybe I should think about how I'd feel climbing two flights of stairs to my apartment when I was a decade older.

I glanced at the time. Cameron had called awfully early to catch me. It was only 6:15 a.m. The realtor's office wouldn't be open for hours. Then the time sunk in and I leapt from my chair. Gina was surely being slammed with the morning rush.

Chapter Two

THE MORNING CAREENED on like an out-of-control freight train. I longed to sit down in a quiet corner with my current sock-in-progress and just knit and think for a while to soothe myself, but that wasn't going to happen anytime soon. I was livid. And the smile I gave my customers was forced instead of genuine.

So, I urged Gina to field the register while I assembled the drinks, which was the opposite of our usual arrangement at this time of day. She shot me a confused look, but went right at it. When Angie clocked in after dropping her kids at school, Gina peeled off to go do her work at the university. Angie and I barely had time to exchange a greeting, though we usually fit in some small talk, mostly about what antics her kids were up to.

On a typical day, business came in waves: surge and recover, surge and recover. But this was one of those days that just wouldn't let up. There were no breaks between customers. We started to run low on some things, and I hoped we'd make it until 10:00 a.m. when one of my part-time college students was due to come in, so they could run up to the second-floor storeroom and bring down some supplies.

"Charlie, phone call for you!" Ethan's Australian baritone called out.

I looked up from tamping down ground coffee in a portafilter. Ethan was there. That meant it was already 10:00 a.m. or after. I continued the motions of making a drink, keeping the customer's choices at the front of my mind so I wouldn't have to waste time glancing at the computer screen again. "Can you take a message?"

Ethan pulled a comical face that made me splutter out a laugh almost against my will. "No can do, Ms. Shaw. They say they've been trying to get ahold of you for a week. They said they'll wait."

I handed a customer his drink, tapped the nearest screen to indicate that order was filled, and turned to Ethan. "Take over —and when I get back I'll need you to do some restocking."

Ethan smiled like he was pleased with himself. "Already did a five-point restock!"

I hurried to my office, noticing that Marilyn, one of my favorite regulars, was talking to a stranger next to the yarn wall, clearly selling her on my yarns. She is such a good egg. We're lucky in that we don't often have yarn customers at the same time as a coffee slam, but when that happens, invariably Marilyn will step in to help, if present. Every time I noticed, I presented her with a generous gift certificate, none of which she'd yet used.

I blew out a breath and sat heavily at my desk. Harvey yawned and groaned, giving me a side eye for disrupting his sleep. "Hello? This is Charlie Shaw. How can I help you?"

"Mrs. Shaw, this is Porter Cole, owner of Cole Coach Lines."

My mind raced. That sounded familiar. Then it kerchunked into place. This was the bus company that I'd hired for the event coming up at the end of the month. They were probably calling to confirm the dates and times. "Yes, Mr. Cole. How are you?" I tried to sound pleasant and not rushed, but I didn't think I was doing a very good job.

"I've been trying to contact you for days. I regret to inform you that I've had to file bankruptcy and I will not be able to provide transportation for your event."

"What?" I sputtered. Something caved inside me, and panic started pouring out.

"Cole Bus Lines is going out of business—"

I realized he was going to repeat the whole thing, which I'd actually heard—I'd just found it unbelievable. "Oh, I'm so sorry," I said lamely. I shouldn't be thinking about how this intensified my own problems. This guy was losing his business, for Pete's sake.

The phone went quiet for a moment as I scrambled to think of something to say or to ask that would be appropriate, but came up empty.

His voice sounded a little bitter now. "Well, all I can say is, online reviews matter, whether they're true or not."

My anger toward Mike Blankenship and his illicit website tampering flared up again from where it had been coaxed down to a smoldering coal over the last few hours. Could the same thing be about to happen to me? This was sudden. Could bad online reviews sour people on a business that fast? I wondered whether there was more to the story, but I decided not to press. "Good advice," I said woodenly. "I'll keep that in mind. All my best to you, Mr. Porter."

"I'm sorry to leave you high and dry. When you check your email, you'll find I've sent you some recommendations for other companies that might be able to help you with your event. They're all aware of what's happened and are working to accommodate our customers."

We said our goodbyes. I grabbed a scrap piece of paper

and wrote down *check email, transportation for Farm Hop ASAP*. I'd been so focused on customer emails I hadn't opened any from anyone else. As soon as I got a moment to breathe, I was going to have to take care of this detail or my event would be a disaster.

A fragment of conversation from the store floated in through the open door and seeped into my thoughts. "This is my favorite yarn to work with," Marilyn rhapsodized. "Charlotte does such a wonderful job with it. Have you heard about these yarns?"

A warm feeling settled over me. I relaxed with my palms on the desk and took a deep breath to slow my heart and my thoughts, to recenter myself. It was going to be okay. As long as I had customers like Marilyn, this business would continue to thrive no matter what the Mike Blankenships of the world did to me.

"I read online that she convinced local sheep farmers to raise special sheep to make yarn," the young woman replied.

A joyful smile spread over my lips. Yep. I'd done that.

"Oh, yes. I'm sure you know about fine Merino wool, but there are so many other wonderful breeds and each has its own characteristics. A longwool breed like the Border Leicester produces a silky and lustrous wool with drape for days. It makes a wonderful scarf or sweater."

I could just imagine Marilyn picking up a jewel-toned skein made from Border Leicester wool and handing it to the young woman. She would squeeze it and be surprised. They always were.

I stood and moved my note to the center of my desk, to attack during a lull later in the day. I needed to let Marilyn get back to her knitting and coffee.

"But is it soft? Oh! It is soft!"

I beamed and headed toward the door.

The young woman continued, softly, "But isn't the owner

kind of flakey? I read online that the store has had a bunch of problems lately."

There was a hitch in my step, but I kept going.

———

AN HOUR later the streams of people finally petered out. I looked out the window for the first time in forever and it had grown into a grim, cloudy midday that was beginning to spit rain. That explained it.

I filled out another gift certificate for Marilyn, made her a fresh coffee, and sat down in a comfy spring-green club chair opposite her. Marilyn is a dark-skinned lady who had retired from her work as a physics professor at EIU and refocused her immense drive into philanthropic work of many types.

Fun, generous, and hella smart, she's been a regular since I opened the store. She's a superb knitter and is always the leader of any charity drive we run, constantly working on hats and mittens for the homeless, caps and blankets for preemies at nearby hospitals, and chemo hats for local cancer centers. She starts nearly every day of the year in that spot, sipping coffee and knitting away for hours at a time before she goes off to do all the other wonderful things she does. I adore her and look forward to seeing her each and every day.

"Busy day," she commented as I placed the fresh coffee and gift certificate within easy reach of her. Neither of us commented on it. We didn't need to. It was an old ritual.

"You don't know the half of it," I said with a chuckle.

I'D JUST FINISHED CALLING all of Cole's recommended alternative bus lines for rates and availability when my sister Rebecca waltzed in. She leaned her hip on one side of the doorframe to my office and rapped her nails on the other. "How about some lunch?" she asked tiredly.

I looked up through the window into the store. Both Ethan and Angie had had a break. We were caught up on stocking, cleaning, and filling online orders. The store was mostly empty and we weren't likely to see many customers until the late-afternoon doldrums hit.

"Yes, but just something quick. I'm swamped."

She rolled her eyes. "So hire more people."

This was an old dance. Rebecca had a lot of opinions. Her heart was in the right place and she'd helped me start this business and make it successful in more ways than I could count. Without her, I couldn't have even gotten a loan as a new divorcee without any credit. She'd taught me how to do the books, helped me choose contractors, and decorate the store. But that had been years ago and she still thought she had a say in how I ran things. True, she had a degree in business and finance, was a vice president at the local bank, and was seldom wrong— but I disliked her presentation.

I kept my voice low so no customers could overhear. "I'd love to, but I can't yet. I'm thinking about buying the building next store and expanding."

She straightened and towered over me. "What? Have you put in an offer? How could you do this without consulting me?" Her voice carried more than I'd like.

I shooed her out of the store and down the street into a little cafe, assuring her I hadn't done anything yet. And then I told her what Cameron at Comp Time had discovered.

She was instantly incensed on my behalf. "The nerve!" she all but shouted. "Well, I can see why you're thinking about buying that property. It would solve the problem once and for all. But that building's a mess. Who knows what you're going to find in those walls?" She curled her lip in disdain.

I nodded. "I know. I know. It's a risk."

"A *huge* risk," she emphasized. "Before you make an offer, have you talked to Glenn Swinarski about the problem?"

Glenn was the top detective on the local police force, and also a regular customer. People teased me that he was sweet on me, but I didn't see any of the signs, and I wasn't in the market anyway. I was focused on the store and long past the days of sighing over boys.

"No," I admitted.

"You should," she insisted. "And consult a lawyer too. Something surely can be done about this."

"I'm worried about it escalating. If he'll do this over a few complaints over noise, what else will he do? I'm afraid to find out."

"Well, don't rush into anything. Good financial decisions are never rushed. I thought you wanted to buy a house? Living in an apartment at your age is for the birds. That would also solve the noise problem for you."

"I do want a house," I said wistfully. "But I've always wanted the store to be bigger too. I can't have both, and right now this seems more important."

The buildings on Main Street were built in the mid- to late 1800s from brick and stone, one right up against the next on every block. Most of the interior spaces are long and narrow, which must have been ideal over a century before but feels a little bit cramped these days. Several merchants on the street have bought two or three buildings and knocked down the walls between, opening their stores up for a more airy, comfortable feeling. The expansion certainly wasn't a revolutionary idea.

Rebecca delved deep into the topics of price and the cost of remodeling as we finished up lunch. As she set her napkin next to her plate, she said, "You would have additional income from the apartments upstairs, assuming they're livable."

I hadn't thought of that. That would offset my costs. It was just one more thing to think about.

As we headed back toward the Tink Tank, the sky opened up. Of course Rebecca had a giant umbrella in her oversized designer purse, and we huddled together as we hurried toward the shelter of the store, me in my comfortable sneakers trying to avoid being pinned under her pointy heels.

Making it into the store was a relief. Until I looked up and my eyes met those of Mike Blankenship. He smiled smugly at me and raised his paper cup of *my* coffee in a mock salute.

Chapter Three

I THINK I stood there gaping for a few seconds. I just couldn't believe he would come in so casually for coffee after what he'd done. Did he think I still didn't know? Did he think I wouldn't find out?

He laughed at my expression, his rough, stubbled face crinkling with glee.

He laughed. At me.

Rage ran hot and cold up and down my spine. I wanted to unleash a torrent of words that would make this twenty-something, tattooed, flannel-wearing, too-handsome-for his-own-good dudebro cower at my feet.

However. I took a deep breath and wrestled inside my brain.

This was not the time or place. I couldn't make a scene. I'm a professional. I have manners, something he clearly didn't know anything about.

Except... I forgot Rebecca was standing behind me.

She did not have the same compunctions, despite her lectures to the contrary.

"You've got a lot of nerve coming in here after what you've done!" Rebecca exclaimed.

I turned and put a hand on her arm. *Gently, gently.* "No, Becca. Let's stay civil."

Her eyes flashed and never left his face. Mike had woken the overprotective bear inside her, and she was going to have some difficulty staying silent. I decided instantly that I'd better get him out of there as fast as possible.

"Mr. Blankenship," I said in a low voice so it wouldn't carry. "You are not welcome here. Please leave and do not come back."

He raised his hands, aping surprise. His unbuttoned flannel shirtsleeve fell back, and I could see a demon peeking out at me on his forearm. Another one glared at me from his neck. "Whoa ho! The little old lady has a voice of her own. That's interesting for a change, isn't it? Speaking for yourself instead of siccing the pigs on me." He looked around like he was expecting the rest of my customers to agree with him.

My fingers started to shake. I didn't want him to know he had me upset so I clenched my hands into fists, nails digging into my palms. "Please leave," I repeated.

He folded his arms over his burly chest like he was settling in for a long stay. He was enjoying this. "I'm not going anywhere. This is too much fun. It's like the white-hair brigade up in here."

"You hacked my online store and I have plenty of documentation to prosecute," I ground out, low enough that I hoped only he would hear.

He didn't follow suit. He crowed, "Good luck with that. Did you think I wasn't going to do anything after you tried to steal my business?"

My brows drew together. He was talking nonsense. I had no plans to open a tattoo parlor. "What are you talking about? How could I possibly steal your business?"

He narrowed his eyes at me under his artfully rumpled hairdo. "How many buildings with low rent do you think there are within walking distance of campus? I'll tell you, since you seem so clueless—none. Yeah, the owner of my building told me he had a possible offer and he told me who it was. You won't be rid of me that easily."

My mouth opened, and I let out an inarticulate sound. I wished the owner had been more discreet. "I was considering expanding my business and wanted to explore my options. You may have noticed I didn't follow through. There was no need for retaliation. We're supposed to be adults."

He guffawed. "Adults know how to do things that kids— and little old grannies—don't. You make it too easy."

He was pushing too hard with the grannie comments. He knew what he was doing, and I was falling for it. My blood was boiling. "That's enough. Just get out."

"No. What are you gonna do about it, grannie? You gonna make me?"

He was so vile.

I didn't even *have* grandchildren yet.

I was breathing so hard it was like I was running a marathon.

"What are we going to do? This is what we're going to do!" Rebecca shouted.

I turned to see she'd pulled a fuchsia canister of pepper spray out of her purse and was aiming it at Mike. *She* wasn't shaking. She looked like she'd just swallowed the fury of three suns.

I tried pushing her arm down, but it wouldn't budge. My mind raced. If she pulled that trigger I'd have to evacuate the store. The police would have to be called. There'd be an incident report. It would show up in the local police blotter. That would be bad for business.

It was like my anger had been doused with ice-cold water.

I could not let that happen.

"Stay calm, Becca. You'll gas the whole store."

"It'll be worth it," she growled.

"Not to me," I replied urgently. "My customers could be hurt."

The store had gone silent, aside from the ambient music we played—gentle techno electronica with soft feminine voices melodiously filling the space was quite a contrast to the static electricity that had built up between the three of us.

Everyone was looking at me to see what I would do.

Then I heard Ethan's Australian twang behind Mike. "Yes, ma'am. We need an officer at the Tink Tank on Main. We have a belligerent customer who's refusing to leave. He's creating a bit of a scene. Yes, that's right. That's the correct address. Thank you." He hung up the phone. "There's an officer two blocks away and he's on his way, Charlie."

Mike snorted. "Typical. Can't fight your own battles, so you gotta call the pig. Whatever." He threw up his free hand and sidled slowly for the door. When he reached it, he said, "Just so you know, I'm not done yet. I have a few surprises left. You'll find out soon enough. That farm thing you have planned is going to be loads of fun for your customers. *Not.*"

He was such a juvenile delinquent. I wanted to punch him.

Rebecca kept the pepper spray aimed at him until the door closed. "And don't come back!"

I sagged.

"Just so everyone present understands what just happened," Rebecca announced loudly, "that's the thug who hacked the Tink Tank website and caused Charlotte a lot of distress."

I sighed heavily. I was sure they'd all just been straining to hear that. They didn't need her to announce it. There was just no stopping her sometimes.

A moment later I noticed Ben Davies approaching me with coffee in hand and an embarrassed look on his face. I bristled nonetheless. Ben and Mike were best friends and had been since high school. Where you found one, you likely found the other—often in bars, getting drunk and rowdy. Or so I'd heard.

Ben was a pretty average fellow. Conventionally handsome. He'd always seemed like such a nice guy, and I had never understood how he could stand spending so much time with Mike. They were like yin and yang, at least from what I'd observed.

Ben came in frequently at this time of day, often buying several coffees at a time for people next door. He'd even spent a considerable amount of time shopping for knitting supplies just a few months before, putting together a beginner's knitting kit for his girlfriend Lauren's birthday. He didn't have much to spend, which he apologized for profusely at the time, because he worked second shift at the local electronics factory and didn't make much. He'd been a perfect gentleman, affable and friendly.

"For what it's worth, I'm sorry, Charlie," Ben said. He shook his head. "I don't know what gets into him sometimes."

I grimaced. I didn't know what to say to that. I would not say it was okay.

Lauren came up behind him with her own coffee. She'd been the recipient of that gift. I wondered fleetingly if she'd ever used it. She'd never come to any of my beginner classes.

She flicked her long, perfectly curled blonde hair over her shoulder and wrapped her free hand around his arm possessively. Her long nails flashed with little gems. "You better get going or you'll be late for your shift," she said, looking up at him adoringly. Then she turned her head to glare at me.

I didn't know what Lauren held against me, but she was almost always in Ben's shadow and never had a kind word or expression for me. I chalked it up to her being the kind of woman who cultivated the perfect makeup, hair, and nails and felt disdain for those of us who forwent such things. I honestly couldn't think of another reason for it.

Ben blinked and pinched the bridge of his nose. "Yeah, yeah. I better go. Just wanted you to know I think he's off base here."

"I've gotta scoot back to the salon too," Lauren cooed. She was a nail technician at a shop down the street called Phalanges. She reached up on tiptoe to bus his lips, her high heels coming up off the floor, then shot me a hateful look and pulled him bodily out of the store by the arm.

I stood there for another moment, still bewildered.

Angie came around the counter with a coffee and the small knitting bag I kept hanging on a peg for quiet moments. She seemed to think I needed to do something soothing.

She wasn't wrong.

Conflict makes me shaky. Because the moment it's over, the worry begins.

Would my customers think less of me? What were they thinking about me and how I handled myself just then? What would they say to their friends when they related this moment? Would they choose a different coffee shop next time so they could avoid the drama?

Had I just torpedoed my business?

What could I have done differently to avoid this outcome?

"Let's go sit for a minute," Angie said as she put her arm around me and guided me toward my office. I was happy to escape.

Harvey stood in the doorway to my office on high alert. The raised voices must have disturbed his nap. He knew he wasn't allowed to come into the store unless I said it was okay, so he hovered there, his warm brown eyes worried. He kept glancing around the store like he was unsure what he should do. As I edged by him into my office, he turned and leaned against me, looking up into my face for direction.

I pulled the blinds across the glass window that overlooked the store, plonked down in my chair, and focused on Harvey. Stroking his soft fur helped my blood pressure go down. I could practically feel it. Becca hovered menacingly in the doorway but was mercifully silent.

"You should go back to work," I said.

"Oh, no. I'm giving a statement before I leave," she retorted.

Glenn Swinarski arrived a few minutes later. I could hear Rebecca giving her statement. I groaned into Harvey's neck over how loud she was being. The coffee and knitting Angie had brought for me went untouched. I was too wound up already to caffeinate myself more, and there was no way I could knit. I'd drop half the stitches.

Angie brought Glenn back to my office when he finished in the store.

I read somewhere once that fifty percent of people go fifty percent grey by the age of fifty. Well, Glenn and I are over-achievers. His is steel grey; mine, solid white. My hair color hadn't concerned me for years. I wore it daily in a long braid down my back for ease. I didn't have the time or inclination to mess with hair dye. Mike's comments about my hair didn't cut me, but his insinuation that I was old… Well, that kinda did.

Of course, it's a different story for men. Lots of women find a silver fox irresistible. After what my ex had put me through—leaving me for a younger woman just as my boys left the nest—I wasn't interested. Maybe I'd change my mind one day. But for now I was too busy to feel lonely.

Harvey was the only man I needed.

Glenn took one look at me, sent me a sympathetic glance, then turned around and came back with a chair from the store. He positioned himself against the wall, holding the lightweight chair high above his head so he could shut the door with his foot. Then he set the chair back down and took a seat. It was cozy.

He started asking questions. I answered him with as much detail as I could.

A knock sounded behind him. Glenn shuffled his chair forward until his knees were brushing mine and raised his eyebrows.

"Come in if you can," I called out, my face flushing hot with embarrassment that my office was so small I couldn't have a private meeting with someone.

A disembodied hand appeared with a coffee for Glenn. He chuckled and took it.

We went over the details. I told him about Mike's tampering with my website as well as his threat against the Farm Hop. Glenn asked if he could talk to Cameron at Comp Time. I told him that was fine.

I tend to notice odd things when under stress. At that moment I could not stop noticing that I couldn't see Glenn's top lip under his enormous, walrusy mustache. I wondered if he thought it made him seem more approachable. Or maybe authoritative?

How did I perceive it?

Comical, I decided. With a dash of cute in a round-faced, baby-animal sort of way. I didn't let on.

"You seem a bit shaken," Glenn said.

"I'm not shaken. I'm angry," I replied.

His brows shot up. By gosh, they were as bushy as the mustache.

"Glenn, I opened this store nine years ago. That's nine years with barely more than a few days off every year. I'm finally at a point where I *might* be able to stop and take a breath. I've been climbing this ladder a long time, and I feel like he just kicked it out from under me."

He leaned forward, making strong eye contact. "I understand, Charlotte, and I'll do what I can." He patted my knee and eased back again. "That said, if I were you I'd do whatever I could to make sure everything's buttoned up nice and tight. Cyber-security-wise and whatnot. And your doors. You got a security system?"

"This is Abingdon, Iowa. I never thought I needed one," I replied.

"Well, I bet old Harvey here will do you just fine. They say dogs are statistically a better deterrent to crime than a security system."

"Do they just say that or is it actually true?" I asked.

He tilted his head and squinted. "You know, I'm not sure. I'll have to get back to you on that."

We both laughed. I liked Glenn. He was a nice guy.

"I'll be warning Blankenship that I'm watching. That's about all I can do at this point. As far as the Internet stuff goes, I'll talk to the county prosecutor, but don't get your hopes up. I don't think Sam has progressed past AOL in that regard." Glenn shrugged and shut his notebook. "You can always hire a lawyer for a civil suit if you can find someone who'll take it, though it'll cost you a pretty penny, I'm sure."

"That's what I hear. Thank you for coming so fast."

He nodded and stood. "Now, if I can just gracefully extricate myself," He shuffled to one side before lifting the chair again, holding it over his head, and grabbing the doorknob quickly before he lost the balancing act. A few seconds later he was gone.

I inhaled deeply. Let that breath out slowly. Harvey continued to look up at me with pleading eyes. I held up my finger, picked up the phone to call my favorite of the bus companies back. That took just a minute.

The Farm Hop later in the month was back on track. Some of my most devoted customers would be flying in from all over the country for it. There was a bus reserved once again to take

them on a tour of local farms, where they could meet individual sheep out in the field in order to decide whether they
wanted to bid on any fleeces to be processed into their favorite
format for spinning or their favorite type of yarn. I had all
kinds of fun activities planned. It was going to be a knitting
and spinning retreat celebrating wool and the camaraderie of
crafters.

Unless Mike Blankenship managed to screw it up.

I popped up from my chair and grabbed Harvey's leash
and my ratty old umbrella. It was time for our afternoon walk.
It would be good to get out of the building, stretch our legs,
and try to forget about Mike's nefarious plans for a few minutes
at least.

Just as I got to the back door that led out to the alley, I
smelled cigarette smoke. Andrea Blankenship, Mike's fraternal
twin sister and business partner, sometimes smoked under my
building's overhang when it rained because their building
didn't have one. It irritated me. Wool and other fibers are
prone to picking up odors easily. The last thing I wanted was to
sell stinky yarn and roving.

I leaned my forehead against the door. Poor Harvey
hopped on his front legs, his tags jingling merrily, eager to go
out. I did *not* want another confrontation.

I checked to make sure the air purifier I kept by the back
door was running and considered going out through the front,
but this was my building and I was going to use it how I
pleased.

I made plenty of noise opening the door so if she was still
out there, she'd know I was coming. The rain had stopped
recently by the looks of it, but the clouds still hung low, grey
and threatening. Harvey barreled out ahead of me, pulling his
leash until it was taut. When I followed, I found him seated in
front of Andrea, who was leaning against the wall smoking.
The back door to Trance was propped open beside her.

From what I could tell, Andrea wasn't much like her brother. I gleaned that Andrea did most of the tattoo work in their shop, while her brother only took on special "art" projects. She was wan and exceedingly thin with deep hollows under her eyes. She exuded weariness. She definitely had a troubled look about her.

And I guess she had reason for that. She was an ex con. It had been a drug charge. Meth. That was the extent of my knowledge on the topic.

Andrea flicked the cigarette away and patted Harvey on the head. She looked up at me, a sad look in her eyes. Her voice was a soft whisper, like she was afraid of being overheard. "I'm really sorry about the crap he's pulling," she said. "I've been trying to talk him out of it, but he's bull-headed."

"Do you know what he's planning to do the weekend of my Farm Hop?" I kept my voice equally low.

She let out a long-suffering sigh. "He's having a sale—ten dollars for a one-hour session—day and night for the entire weekend. He's advertising it to biker gangs, mostly." Her eyes cut away from me, her disgust and annoyance with the whole thing obvious.

I tried not to panic. So there'd be motorcycles parked on the street. That didn't necessarily mean anything. "So you'll all be here around the clock the whole weekend?"

She tapped a pack of cigarettes in the palm of her hand with a frown on her face. "Well, I will be. I don't know about anyone else."

A yell came through Trance's open back door. Mike's voice. "Andrea! Customer!"

Her lip curled in a snarl. "He's playing a video game right now and can't be bothered." She pushed herself away from the wall with a foot and trudged inside.

The clouds chose that moment to pour buckets down on us.

Chapter Four

THE RAIN KEPT up all night, muting any sounds that might have originated from the neighboring building. I counted that as a blessing and snuggled down for the evening under a fluffy afghan with Harvey draped over my feet. I lit a few candles, poured a glass of wine, pulled out a mindless knitting project, and caught up on one of my favorite television shows.

Indie space-dyed yarns were my favorite—the more bright colors, the better. Watching the colors slip through my fingers and coalesce into mesmerizing patterns under my needles never failed to lift my mood.

I suspected there was a unicorn somewhere in my lineage. Some people were all about the shine and sparkle—gold, silver, gems. Not me. All I ever wanted was to be surrounded with every color in the rainbow, preferably all at once.

I smiled to myself. I'd achieved that. Both my shop and my home were cheerful and bright.

I tried not to think about the fact that the Farm Hop was just a few weeks away and that Mike Blankenship was going to do his best to spoil our fun. There was nothing I could do about that, and there was little to gain by worrying about something I couldn't control.

When the time came, I'd make the best of it. Raising two boys had taught me a lot about improvising and staying loose and open to possibilities instead of dwelling on the negative. If I hadn't learned to be flexible, to pivot when something wasn't working, I doubted my boys would have turned out so awesome. This attitude had served me well in my business, and I knew it was one of my strengths. The Farm Hop was going to be great.

All too soon my eyes grew heavy behind my progressive lenses. Harvey and I padded downstairs for one more quick bathroom break before settling down and falling asleep to the pitter-patter of rain on the roof.

I WOKE up three minutes before my alarm was set to go off, feeling optimistic and ready to tackle the day. I flipped on the light and eased my legs over to sit on the edge of the bed. One of my first thoughts was about calling the real estate agent to get the ball rolling on buying the building next door. I raised my eyebrows and blinked. If that was what my gut told me after sleeping on it, that was probably what I should do.

As usual, no part of Harvey moved from his spot on the bed, aside from his eyes following me while I performed my daily ablutions and fixed a light breakfast of scrambled eggs with some cheddar cheese and a piece of bacon thrown in. I'd have my coffee downstairs. I ate quickly, threw on a jacket, and picked up a leash. The jingle brought Harvey to my side in a flash.

As we walked down the narrow stair past Gina's apartment, I heard her singing and pots and pans clattering. I wasn't the only one in a great mood.

When I threw open the back door, a wave of frigid, moist

air hit me. The temps had managed to stay above freezing overnight, but it was still uncomfortably cold. I peered out into the dim light from the safety lamp. It wasn't raining at the moment, but it smelled like more could be coming anytime, so I fumbled with the coat rack on the wall for my umbrella.

Harvey, already a few steps outside, whined and pulled at the leash. That wasn't like him at all. He normally waited patiently just a step away, even when he really had to go. I frowned and tucked the closed umbrella under my arm.

Something outside had caught his attention. Maybe a squirrel or a cat was lingering in the alley? He'd never chased one before. Most Great Pyrenees were content to simply sniff and watch. A low prey drive was critical in a breed that was developed to blend in with a flock of sheep and watch over them in the field, not to herd them. It wouldn't do to have them chasing lambs when they were supposed to keep the sheep from being eaten by wolves. Harvey came from a long line of working flock protectors. I'd first met him as a thirteen-week-old puppy on a local sheep farm. He'd grabbed my heart that day and he'd been my best friend since.

Harvey suddenly lunged, tugging on my arm so hard I dropped the umbrella. I fought for control of the dog, exhorting him to be good while I bent over and picked it up. I spotted a flashlight I kept near the door and grabbed it as I followed Harvey's insistent tugs out the door.

"What are you all in a fluff about?" I demanded.

My eye followed the direction he was pulling. I squinted. Was there someone over there? I could see a shape next to the big blue dumpster. Was it someone Harvey knew? That might explain his eagerness. He is never more animated than when he's about to get loved on.

I let him drag me forward, but slowly. I could make out a human form. They seemed to be sitting on a chair. In the alley.

Next to the dumpster that served all the businesses on this block.

I frowned. Sitting on a chair in an alley next to a dumpster at five thirty in the morning was pretty odd.

Could it be a Trance customer taking a break from their tattoo session? I glanced at the building next door. It was shuttered up, and I didn't see any light coming from the small ground-floor window on this side.

"Hello?" I called and drew forward a few steps. Something wasn't quite right. The person wasn't moving. They seemed to be slumped forward a little.

No one answered. I swallowed convulsively. A cold feeling spread through my body. My fingertips tingled.

Maybe someone on the block had thrown out a chair, and a homeless person had decided to have a rest there? Could they be sleeping?

It was awfully cold at night to be sleeping outside. Maybe they needed help.

Could it be an old, discarded store mannequin that was freaking Harvey out? I'd feel pretty silly if it was that simple.

Something told me it wasn't.

A fresh wave of fear washed over me. I hesitated for a moment, rooted where I stood. Harvey continued to whine and pull toward the seated figure.

I turned on my flashlight. Reflected light bounced back from the head area. Plastic? I couldn't see much else. The flashlight was too dim.

Now I was truly stumped. Curiosity got me moving forward again. What on Earth was I seeing?

I crossed the final ten feet.

And screamed.

It took me about three seconds to recover. Sliding the leash up my arm, I dropped the umbrella and flashlight to dig a box cutter out of my jeans pocket. Then I cut through the rope around the person's neck and pulled the plastic bag away from their face.

It was Mike Blankenship.

My fingers shook as I searched for a pulse. I felt nothing. But I didn't know for sure. His body seemed cold to me. But I was cold too. I wasn't an expert. I'd just taken a few classes in CPR because I felt like it was my civic duty when working with the public. I'd never had live experience. But there was no one else to turn to. I had to do this.

I knew this man. And though I disliked him, I certainly didn't want him dead.

I didn't know how long he'd been like this. Was he already gone? If there was a chance I could save him, I had to try.

My thoughts were like lightning flashes. I was doing things almost before I was fully aware of them. I had the chair on the ground and started compressions and I didn't even think about how heavy he was. Adrenaline had taken over and I was on autopilot.

"Charlie? Are you okay?"

I glanced up as I counted compressions. It was Gina, standing at the back door in sweats and a bathrobe. I blew a breath into Mike's lungs and called out to her. "Come get my phone from my pocket and call 911."

"Oh… God," she murmured, but quickly did as I asked. She also slid the leash off my arm and hovered nearby with Harvey, who had finally calmed down.

Vincent came out of his shop a moment later with a full trash bag in his hand. He said and did little, just staring at me working like he was dazed. Something niggled at me that his reaction was odd, but there was no time to dwell on it.

Tiny pebbles dug into my knees. My back and legs ached from the awkward position, but I ignored it and kept up the CPR.

Gina stood vigil with me. Her phone was on speaker and

the police dispatcher stayed on the line, helping me count compressions and breaths. I couldn't look at Mike's face while I worked. It was too awful. I tried not to think about it. He might be dead, but since I wasn't sure, I knew I couldn't stop.

It seemed like it took forever for police to arrive. One of them, a young man I didn't know well, took Mike's pulse, shook his head, and grimaced, but he took over the CPR. I stumbled back out of the way gratefully.

Gina put her arm around me protectively as the other officer questioned me about what I'd found, when, and whether I'd felt a pulse before I started compressions. His manner was detached and remote. It seemed so strange in the face of what was happening at our feet.

I felt numb. The cold seeped into me all the way down to my bones. I started to shiver and my teeth chattered as I spoke. Gina went into the building and brought out an afghan to wrap around me. I appreciated the gesture, but it didn't help at all.

The ambulance arrived a couple of minutes later. Then another two police cars and a fire truck pulled up behind it. The alley was packed with vehicles and people. The officers guided us back toward the building. Gina, Vincent, and I huddled together in the puddle of light coming out of the Tink Tank's back door as one of the officers began to rope off the alley with police tape.

The paramedics took Mike's pulse, shined a light in his eyes, and hooked up leads to his body while someone maintained CPR. They spoke quietly with the police officers. After a few minutes they stopped the CPR. One of them got on her cell phone. Her expression was grim. She was only a few steps away from us. There wasn't anywhere else for her to go.

"Hi, Dr. Ahmed. Sorry if I woke you. This is Paramedic Schmidt with Heartland Ambulance Service unit number four. We need you at a crime scene downtown."

Gina turned huge eyes on me. Dr. Ahmed was well known. He was a beloved local veterinarian who had been reelected to the office of coroner election after election.

The paramedic glanced at us and turned away, but I could still hear her. "Pupils are fixed and dilated. Absent heart tones. Asystole in all three leads. The body is cold. No rigor yet. CPR was given for at least twenty minutes, but I think he's been dead for a while."

I turned my head into Gina's shoulder and felt a few tears slip down my cheeks. She squeezed me tight. I was glad she was there with me. For the first time in a very long time, I didn't want to be alone.

Chapter Five

WE DIDN'T OPEN the store. I couldn't smile at customers and make lattes after what had just happened. I couldn't ask Gina to do that either. It didn't seem right. For the first time in nine years, the Tink Tank was closed on a day that wasn't Thanksgiving or Christmas.

Gina did make coffee for the professionals working in the alley, after she walked Harvey for me and took him upstairs. She loaded up a tray with steaming paper cups and passed them out. The sun was just coming up and it was a cold spring morning. I was sure the hot drink was a welcome comfort.

It felt weird to sit at a table in the back of the darkened store. We left the main lights off to let our early customers know we weren't open. The light in my office was on, though, which was enough to make me feel safe. I had my hands wrapped around a cooling mug of coffee and the afghan still draped over my shoulders when Glenn Swinarski came in. He pulled out a chair near mine and sat down, his brow creased. He sighed. "How you holding up?"

"Okay, I think," I said. "I've never… " My voice wavered, and I trailed off because I didn't want to say the words.

He nodded. "I bet not. It's a shock to the system. We don't see much like this around here. You did a good job. You did what was right."

My eyes were watery. I dashed the tears away with cold fingertips. They felt like a weakness.

"Now, I know this is soon, Charlotte, but I've got some questions to ask you."

I let out a shaky breath. I'd already told the officers what I knew, but the police seemed to like redundancy, and it didn't hurt me to repeat myself. "Go ahead."

"The yarn that was wrapped around his throat—is that one you sell here?"

I frowned. "Yarn?"

"You didn't notice it was yarn?"

"It was dark. I wasn't paying attention to what the fiber was. I just wanted to get the bag off his head so he could breathe."

"That what you'd call it? A fiber?"

I took a deep breath to calm myself a little. "Yes, to distinguish the source material. There's cotton, linen, hemp, and rayon of different types, and those are all plant fibers. Acrylic and nylon are manmade. Of course rayon is manmade, too, but we don't need to get into the weeds. Then there's wool, silk, mohair, alpaca, and so on, which are animal-based fibers."

He slid a baggie from an inside pocket of his coat. It was obvious that it contained the strands I'd cut from Mike's throat. I think my eyes bulged. In the dark they'd registered as grey rope. But now, in the light coming from my office, I could see what they were. A worsted weight cotton-acrylic blend in neon pink.

"Yes, we sell that yarn." I rose, shrugging off the afghan, and walked to the front of the store. Enough light came through the front window that I was able to pick out a fifty-gram ball in the same shade. I brought it back and handed it to Glenn.

The murderer had used yarn, possibly from my store, to kill Mike Blankenship. And they'd chosen well. This was the kind of yarn people used to knit and crochet dishcloths. It was as strong as rope and wore like iron.

But why? Why would they do that? Were they trying to frame me? Was it some kind of message?

And the placement of his body. It seemed like I was the one meant to find him, assuming the killer knew my daily routine. I shuddered. That was a creepy thought. But I didn't push it away. I'd just found a man carefully murdered and left in the alley behind my shop and home. Scenarios I would've called paranoid the day before suddenly seemed appropriate

Glenn turned into the light, examining the ball of yarn closely alongside the contents of his bag. He turned back to me. "I'm no yarn expert, but I'd say that's a match. This stuff sold in a lot of places, or is it unique to your store?"

I shrugged. "It's an inexpensive yarn and people buy a lot of it. Lots of stores carry it. I don't know if anyone else in town has it, but that would be easy enough to check. Of course it's readily available online as well."

His lower lip disappeared completely under his enormous mustache. "I'll have to verify all that," he said slowly, shooting me an apologetic look.

I went still. "What do you mean?"

"I mean don't leave town, for now."

I blinked. "Glenn, are you saying I'm a suspect?"

He held up a hand. "It's a formality. No need to get excited. I'm not arresting you. It's my job to chase down all the details. And you did have a confrontation with the deceased just yesterday. And ongoing conflicts, dating back years. If I didn't investigate that, I wouldn't be worth my salt."

I sank back down in my chair and just stared at him.

I was a suspect in a murder investigation. Right after trying to revive a dead man—a man who might have been killed with my yarn. I couldn't believe this was happening.

Glenn stood, holding the baggie and the skein. "Any chance I can take this with me for reference?"

I waved my arms at him. The wholesale price was under a dollar. "Keep it. It's yours."

He slipped them into his coat. "We'll check for prints on the bag and the chair. I'll need you to come down and give us a set."

A wave of nausea washed over me. "You know I touched the bag, Glenn. I had to get it off his head."

"Of course you did. And so did the murderer. It's a process of elimination. Statistically, a good print is a one-in-one-hundred shot. If we get one, we'll need to know if it's yours or someone else's."

"Okay." That explanation helped. A little. I still didn't like the idea of being on the list of suspects.

He leaned in, resting his knuckles on the table. "Charlie, I like you, but I can't play favorites. I don't think it's possible for you to do something like this. I don't believe it's in you. But I have to follow the rules."

I exhaled. "I understand. Do you think I could be in any danger?"

He sniffed and straightened. "You have any enemies in common with Blankenship?"

I recoiled. "No—I don't have any enemies at all!"

"There's your answer."

He seemed to be disengaging, so I asked reflexively, "Is there anything I can do to help?"

"You just live your life. I know this morning was rough. Try not to dwell on it. Put it behind you. It's no secret that Blankenship wasn't a popular guy. Don't worry. We'll find our man. That's what the City of Abingdon pays us to do." He sauntered toward the back, then stopped. "Let's keep the yarn detail between us. I'd prefer it if you didn't talk to the press at all. And if you could get me a list of people who purchased this yarn in the last six months, I'd be much obliged."

I nodded my assent and he left.

I crossed my arms and put my head down on the table. I wanted to go upstairs and curl into a ball around Harvey, but I felt I should stay on the main floor until the police were done, in case they needed anything.

I started to think about some of the last words Glenn had said before walking out.

We'll find our man.

I don't know why that stood out to me, except that, in general, men seemed to like Mike Blankenship. Maybe they were oblivious to his vile nature, or maybe he was just nicer to them.

Women, on the other hand—especially young women— tended to be disgusted by him once they got to know his reputation. I always hired kids from the university to work for me, so I heard all the gossip whispered around the espresso machine. Though he'd been nearly thirty, Mike had liked to go to campus fraternity parties to pick up young women, which was probably fairly easy for him to do, with that bad-boy heart-throb look young women swoon for.

The rumor was that he'd kept a mattress in the back room of his shop and sometimes slept with women there while customers were being inked by his sister in the front. He also had a reputation for sleeping with his buddies' girlfriends. Supposedly he'd even boasted about it, though I'd never heard it with my own ears. I'd kept my distance from the guy whenever possible.

On second thought, maybe he *had* made some male enemies that way. That could easily be a motive for murder. I know I'd felt pretty awful when my ex had left me. I hadn't felt like murdering anyone, but I'd been pretty darn angry.

But would a man use *yarn* to kill another man with? That detail struck me as odd. Yes, there were male knitters in Abingdon, but not many. What were the chances that some dude in Mike's circle was also a knitter who grabbed the easiest string to hand from his yarn stash when planning to commit murder? And neon pink to boot? Those odds seemed pretty slim to me.

Crafters were makers, not destroyers. A knitter wasn't likely to be a murderer. At least none of the kinds of knitters I'd ever met—and I'd met a lot. Besides, that old bumper sticker was true: *I knit so I don't kill people.* I'd made a drawer full of socks just after my ex's love affair had come to light.

My thoughts were going in circles, round and round, as I tried to make sense of it all. I was weary and probably not in the best frame of mind to come to any steady conclusions.

Why would a non-knitter choose to use my yarn to murder someone? I was sure they'd done that for a reason. I didn't know what that reason was.

But the murderer had involved me with that choice. And that was terrifying.

Chapter Six

ANGIE OPENED the store at nine fifteen after she dropped off her kids at school. She said she didn't mind and wouldn't know what to do with herself if she didn't. So I agreed to let her do it. She phoned up the other part-timers, and together they found a way to fill in all the shifts for the rest of the day.

Gina and I huddled on my sofa upstairs watching television, knitting and sipping hot drinks. It was routine for us to spend evenings like this after closing the store. That day it was more about coping.

I was glad she wanted to stay close. I needed her company as much as she needed mine. Honestly, we didn't know what else to do. There isn't exactly a social protocol for how to behave after finding an acquaintance dead and trying in vain to revive them.

We didn't talk for the longest time, just knitting side by side. I was working on a new pattern that I hoped I had finally gotten right, a Möbius strip cowl, worked in a gradual color-shift silk-and-merino yarn that changed slowly from green to blue and then into purple. The Möbius cast on was daunting for first-timers, but there were videos online that walked through it at a digestible pace, and I hoped my clients would like it, if they could get past that hurdle. I don't know the math behind the Möbius strip, but the mysterious loop with its 180 degree twist that made it a continuous surface without beginning or end had always fascinated me.

There were many patterns similar to this online and in books, but though they were often labeled as cowls, they frequently turned out big enough to be shawls, and knitters ended up looping them around their necks more than once. From my point of view, that defeated the purpose of going to all the trouble of making a true Möbius, because that intriguing twist just got hidden in the folds. I hoped I'd solved that problem by carefully developing the pattern. Once this model was done for the store, I'd make up some kits and see how they would sell.

The soft yarn slipped through my fingers effortlessly, a luxurious comfort. It was a fast and easy project, once you mastered the cast on and joined for an unusual sort of circular double-loop knitting. Then it was just round and round in a simple pattern, alternating between knit and purl each double-loop to make a garter stitch. The bold, horizontal nature of garter stich combined with the gradient-dyed yarn and the twist of the Möbius was shaping up to be a stunning combination, highlighting each choice I'd made so that the finished product would exceed the sum of its parts. The cowl developed from the inside out—both ends at once—which felt magical beneath my fingers.

This project made me feel like a knitting genius. It was the perfect distraction.

I was grateful I had a simple pattern on my needles at the moment. I couldn't handle anything too complex right then. My thoughts were too crowded already. Gina and I silently worked in parallel, both of us lost in our heads.

But as the streaming service was loading the next show in

the series we were watching, Gina leaned forward and pressed pause, then sat back, staring straight ahead, her knitting in her lap. I could barely see her face, which was shrouded by her straight bob falling forward.

"What's wrong?" I asked.

She chewed on her lip but she didn't turn her head to look at me.

"Gina, are you okay?" I myself was feeling like the whole thing hadn't been real. It had the blurred sensation of a dream now. I was probably in a little bit of shock, I supposed. Only time and everyday activity would return my mood back to normal.

Finally she spoke. "I know it's supposed to be sad that someone we know and saw routinely just died. That was a horrific way to go."

I knew instantly what she meant.

She pushed her dark hair from her face and it fell back, sliding smoothly through her fingers. "But... crap on a cracker... "

I think if I hadn't been around, she would have cursed, but she respected my rule of no cursing in the store, even in my apartment. I waited to see what she would say.

"Mike was an awful person. And some part of me thinks he may have gotten what he deserved," she said, barely above a whisper.

I nodded once. We both knew these were taboo sorts of things to think, much less say, and I guess that's what made us speak in hushed voices. "I feel the same way," I said. "I can't stop wondering who did it. That seems more important than anything else."

"Right?" she exclaimed. "This is a pretty small city. Sure, students come and go all the time, but we know almost everyone who lives around here. If we don't know their names, we definitely know their faces."

"At least in the downtown area," I agreed. "Which means we probably know the murderer. I've had the same thoughts. It's a scary feeling." I didn't add my biggest concern—that the murderer had to have used yarn from my store purposefully as a message of some kind. I didn't want to scare her even more. We were both freaked out plenty and Glenn had asked me to keep quiet about that. But it bothered me a great deal. I couldn't stop thinking about it.

She took a sip of her tea. "At first I thought maybe it was one of the young women from the university that he messed around with, but then I realized that just doesn't seem likely."

"What makes you say that?" I asked.

"I don't think women that age generally have the mental resources for something like that. They spend most of their time reacting, getting by. Being in college is overwhelming enough. That's taking up all their time. When something awful happens to a person that age, they tend to shut down and leave school. I see it happen every semester to all kinds of people. It just seems unlikely they'd go to all that trouble for revenge. I mean, that murder was planned."

"What if they were pregnant?"

Gina's eyes widened. "Kill the father and any hope of support when your future is so uncertain?"

"True," I conceded. "But the hormones of pregnancy can sometimes make one a little bonkers. Believe me, I know. If men were the ones who got pregnant, we'd never have survived as a species."

"Maybe." She looked unconvinced. "Have you thought about who might have done it?"

I let out a heavy sigh. "That's all I've been thinking about since they pronounced that he was gone."

"And?"

I slid my eyes sideways over to Gina, evaluating whether I

should confess my thoughts. "I can't stop wondering if Mike did something that finally pushed his sister over the edge."

Gina looked surprised. "Andrea? I don't think so."

"Why not? She clearly doesn't like working for him. He treats women horribly. Maybe he treats her the same way. I get the feeling he doesn't pay her a fair share. This way she inherits the shop and keeps doing what she's always done, without him making everything so hard."

"I don't think she'd do anything that would get her put back in jail, no matter how awful he was to her."

I frowned. "Why do you think that?"

"We're kinda friends."

I picked up my knitting again and knit a few stitches, thinking about what Gina had said. Her opinion was a strong influence on my thoughts. I knew she was a good judge of character. "I didn't know you knew her."

"Not super well. We talk a little bit from time to time when we see each other out back. She mentioned she was struggling with the English portion of her GED, so I offered to tutor her. We did several sessions. I had to teach her how to read critically and the basics of how to write an essay. No one had ever taught her that before but she picked it up fast. She's very bright. She ended up acing that portion of the test."

I patted her hand and smiled. "You're so wonderful. And such a good teacher! I'm glad you did that."

Gina lit up a little. "She was really grateful and really nice about the whole thing. She offered to pay me with my choice of tattoo and I was tempted, but… "

"You decided you don't want any ink?"

"No, it wasn't that. You're right that Mike didn't pay her fairly. He gave her a small commission for each job and kept the lion's share for himself. I've always wanted to get some ink. And I really want some of her art on my body, but I want to pay full price and I want it all to go to her. So I've been saving up and planned to ask her to do it when he wasn't there."

I was surprised, but I guess I shouldn't have been. Gina had never mentioned to me that she wanted a tattoo. I hoped it wasn't because she thought I wouldn't approve. I didn't want her to see me that way.

Blech.

I work with and serve young people all day long. I know I'm not hip or anything, but I don't want to be seen as an old fuddy-duddy. I think multigenerational groups of people— groups of all kinds of people with different backgrounds and skin tones and cultures—have a lot to offer each other. I guess I just want to be *relevant*.

She shrugged. "There were some really weird family dynamics going on there. Maybe because they were fraternal twins. I don't know. It seemed to me like she felt it was her job to try to keep him out of trouble, which meant she put up with a lot of his bull. She didn't make much working for him and she was pretty unhappy, but she's also been motivated to make her life better. Now that she has her GED, she wants to take classes at the community college in Stafford and hopes eventually to transfer to EIU to major in art. You should see some of her work! She's so talented, and I think she'll do well if she can find a way to afford it. She told me that those years in jail were her low point. She's still trying to crawl out of that hole. I just can't see her putting herself back in that place. It's the absolute last thing she'd ever want to do."

"Hm." I trusted Gina's opinion, but I wasn't ready to cross Andrea Blankenship off the list I was forming in my head just yet. "Do you have any ideas?"

"Ink gone wrong? What if he misspelled something? No regerts?" She slid me a sly smile.

I chortled. "Maybe. I'm sure Glenn will be looking into that as a possibility."

We got lost in our thoughts and stitches, and after a few minutes, she reloaded our TV program. We didn't talk about Mike Blankenship or his sister any more that morning or afternoon, but I wasn't done thinking about who might have looped those strands of yarn around his neck. And why.

Chapter Seven

JUST BEFORE FIVE, Rebecca called and offered to take me out for dinner. She said I needed a treat after the horrible day I'd had, though I was pretty sure she just wanted the inside scoop to give her the edge in tomorrow's office gossip. I demurred. I was pretty comfy in my PJs and didn't want to leave home. Not to mention that the entire neighborhood would waylay us to ask questions about the morning's events. So she volunteered to bring over my favorite takeout instead. It was generous, considering her dislike of Indian food. I took her up on it.

As soon as Gina heard Becca was on her way over, she decided to head back down to her place to "kill some orcs, therapeutically." Video games were her vice, and probably one of the reasons that completing her Ph.D. was taking so long.

I tried to convince her to stay and share a meal with us, but she wasn't interested. My sister made her feel edgy, so I didn't blame her. Sometimes Becca made me edgy too.

Becca breezed in and set several steaming bags on the coffee table, then doffed her coat and flitted into the kitchen for plates and serving utensils. She doesn't believe in eating anything out of Styrofoam. Personally I'd rather not do extra dishes if I don't have to, but I humored her.

The takeout smelled of warm, earthy spices and fried things. Heavenly. Rice and potatoes and fried bread were just what I needed—carb therapy. It looked like she'd ordered a little bit of everything. I was glad to see she remembered what my favorite dishes were. She said very little and served me before herself. I had to admit, it was nice to be the one someone pampered for a change.

I curled up, leaning back with my feet under me, my plate held just under my nose. Oh, how I loved creamy chicken korma. "Ahh," I sighed. "Perfect."

Becca perched on the edge of the sofa with her plate on the coffee table, very ladylike, and cut up a samosa with knife and fork, continental-style. She could be so pretentious sometimes. I was surprised to see her eating anything breadlike. She'd sworn off refined carbs years before "to hang onto her girlish figure." I'd never had such qualms. After having children any thought of trying to stay slim and sexy seemed ludicrous. I'd never been sexy anyway. I valued comfort over appeal toward the opposite gender.

Becca had also gotten herself tandoori chicken and some chana masala, which seemed more like her. I filched a few bites of each for myself. She didn't even bat an eye.

I powered through about a third of my plate before saying much. "Gosh, Becca, thank you. I didn't even realize how hungry I was."

She slid her plate forward on the coffee table gingerly, glancing at Harvey for a second to make sure he wouldn't go after it. He had barely even looked up when she came in with all that food. My boy had good manners and she knew it, but she didn't like dogs. She thought they were too messy. And she was always wary around Harvey, though he'd never given her any reason to be.

She eyed me with exaggerated sympathy. "You poor dear. You must be in shock."

Her overly solicitous attitude grated a little, but I wasn't going to call it out and look a gift horse in the mouth. Her intentions were good, and she'd been kind. I worried my lower lip between my teeth. Suddenly my eyes filled up with tears. I sniffed as a wave of emotion hit me, a futile attempt at holding it back. "A little," I said.

I don't know what it was. Maybe because of how thoughtful she'd been? But the floodgates opened. Suddenly I was sobbing. And half forming words because my throat contracted so hard I couldn't get them out.

She took my plate, set it aside, and kicked off her heels. Then she crawled up next to me, ignoring her pencil skirt, and enveloped me in a tight hug while I heaved and whimpered. "You don't have to be strong all the time."

And she meant it.

I got all the blubbering out. It felt good to release all the pent-up emotion that'd been building all day. It wasn't that I couldn't be emotional in front of Gina. It had just felt like I had to play a more motherly role to her and be strong. But with Becca I could let my guard down. I hadn't even known I'd needed that to happen until it did.

I'd never been one to be dramatic or to emphasize my own needs, and maybe that's why it never occurred to me. Maybe this was one of the lessons of aging. I wasn't the mother of small children anymore. I didn't have anyone to protect from outrageous displays of strong emotion that could cause undue stress or worry. I could just feel it and be done with it instead of letting it fester in silence and solitude. I don't know why sharing it or having a witness made the experience so much more cathartic, but it did.

Suddenly I realized how important having this time with Becca was. I'd been so wrapped up in the store for so long, I'd made little time for my sister, or anyone else for that matter, aside from evenings with Gina after we closed the store—and even then our conversations were often focused on the shop. With my boys so far away, time with family and friends had gotten completely gobbled up by the Tink Tank. Sure, it was understandable. Starting a business was difficult.

But maybe it was time to take a step back and reassess. The store was making money now, a modest but comfortable income. I didn't need to force myself to be there every minute of every day anymore. Perhaps room could be made for more social contact. Some time to laugh and cry. A chance to share my burdens, large and small. To be happier, more balanced, less worried about everything.

Why did it take someone dying for me to realize this?

I went through half a box of tissues mopping myself up. And I felt better. Lots and lots better.

A sigh shuddered out of me. "Thank you."

Becca's eyes were glossy, and now that I looked closely, a little bloodshot. And there was very little eye makeup left on her face. She'd done some crying too. She dabbed delicately at her nose. "I was so worried for you today, but I couldn't get away until five. I'm sorry about that."

"It's okay. I'm glad you're here now." I grabbed her hand and squeezed.

The corner of her mouth turned up in a wobbly smile and she gestured at the food, which we'd barely dented. "More? Or should I wrap this up and bring out phase two?"

My brow creased. "What's phase two?"

She grinned and began to close up the Styrofoam boxes. "This keeps well, yes? You can have some tomorrow. I doubt you'll feel like cooking."

"I never feel like cooking," I said flatly.

She arched a brow. "Neither do I."

She stuffed the leftovers in my fridge, which had been very

sad and empty, then produced another bag that I hadn't noticed before, as well as two spoons.

"Oh my gosh—yes!" I cried, flinging my arms in the air like a spectator at a football game.

A decadent pint of ice cream for each of us in our favorite flavors, the same ones we'd indulged in as teenagers. They had softened while we were eating, and the first bite was perfect. Slightly melty around the edge of the container, but easy to scoop up and soooo creamy. Chunks of rich, dark chocolate melted on my tongue, and juicy cherries with tiny, sugary shards of ice crunched and gushed between my teeth. The best.

"Does Glenn have any suspects?" she asked.

I'd expected these questions much sooner and I'd dreaded them, but at the moment they didn't feel bad, and I didn't mind talking about it. "Not that he's sharing with me," I replied.

"He's got his job cut out for him," she remarked dryly. "Mr. Blankenship was not well liked."

I nodded.

"He'll be remiss if he doesn't take a good hard look at Vincent Pradel," she commented, some of her pretension rising again. "It's always the quiet ones."

"Vincent?" I exclaimed. "No, I don't think so. He's sweet as pie."

"And six months ago Mr. Blankenship utterly crushed him. Publicly. In front of the whole world. That's not the kind of humiliation a person just gets over. The fact that he had to see him and put up with his bad behavior day after day might have cracked him."

I frowned. She wasn't wrong about that. Someone had spray-painted a gay slur on the front window of Vincent's shop. It wasn't much of a stretch to assume it had been one of Mike's clients. When he'd gone in to complain about the vandalism, Vincent hadn't known that Mike had multiple webcams mounted inside his shop for posting videos to YouTube about his business.

Mike had sneered at him, thoroughly dressing Vincent down, attacking on every possible front, until Vincent was visibly shaking and shedding tears. Then Mike had posted the entire confrontation online. It had gone viral. It was the lowest of the low. Online, people called Vincent "Viral Vinnie" and used stills of his facial expressions from the video in horrible memes. Six months later I still occasionally saw those images circulating on social media. And I didn't doubt people still sniggered behind their hands in public whenever he was present.

At the time, Vincent closed up his shop and papered over the windows. It seemed like he was closing down for good. For two weeks he was unreachable. Then one day he reopened and everything had changed. All the bright pink and sparkle was gone from his shop. It was decorated in grey and muted colors with traditional accents instead of fanciful ones. Vincent's comb-over was also gone. He had grown a neatly-groomed beard. And instead of sporting his normal pink-and-purple dress shirts with outrageous bow ties, he'd transformed his wardrobe as well, wearing only conservative colors, traditional ties, always topped with an impeccable white apron.

There was no doubt in my mind that the experience had deeply hurt him. He refused to talk about it, clamming up and finding an excuse to leave if I even gently asked him how he was doing. It seemed the only way to approach him was to pretend nothing had happened and not to comment on the changes.

Could he have spent the last six months planning to murder Mike for revenge?

I felt like I knew him, but did I really? I saw him every day, which gave the illusion that I knew him well, but when I thought about it, our conversations never amounted to much more than small talk. I didn't know where he lived. I didn't know who his friends were or even if he had a partner. Truth be told, I wasn't even sure he was gay, though I'd always sort of assumed. That realization made me ashamed of myself.

I let out a pent-up breath. "Wow. I don't like thinking about people I know this way."

"People?" Becca turned to me, her gaze as focused as a hawk who's spotted prey, her spoon hovering partway to her lips. "Who do you think did it?"

I held up my finger, unwilling to hurry the mouthful of decadence melting on my tongue. "I thought it might be his sister, Andrea, but Gina knows her and doesn't think so."

"Once a felon, always a felon," Becca said, her brows arched. She was artfully digging around for a candy tidbit in her carton. "I'm sure she'll make the short list."

"It won't be easy to narrow it down. Mike did a lot of damage in his short lifetime."

"Karma at its finest," she said dryly. "Whoever it was, they did the world a favor."

I leaned forward and touched her arm. I'd been hesitating to tell Becca this, but two heads were better than one and she was sharp as a tack. "If I tell you something, will you promise not to mention it to anyone else?"

Her head swung back and her features once again displayed her concern. She covered my hand with her own. "Of course."

"The murderer used yarn from my shop to do it," I said, barely above a whisper.

Becca's eyes bulged. She stared at me for a long moment. Then she grabbed the carton of ice cream out of my hands and shoved both containers in the freezer. "Pack a bag. Right now, Charlotte. You're coming home with me."

She threw her coat over her arm and stood there, waiting.

"What? Why?"

"You can bring Harvey. Don't argue with me. My house is like Fort Knox. There's nowhere safer. Start packing."

She'd called him Harvey. Not The Mutt. Or The Furball. She'd never let him into her house before.

She was serious.

I started to protest, but she cut me off. "The risk may be small, but we don't know that for sure. You and your boys are everything to me. I know I don't show that often enough, but in this case, I'm putting my foot down. I'm not taking any chances. If Dan and Blain were here, they'd agree with me."

Her words were kind, but her voice and expression were like a drill sergeant's. It was a low blow mentioning my boys. I didn't get to see them enough because their jobs had taken them both across the country.

"I have to work, Becca. There's still risk."

"During the daytime. With lots of other people around. I will not have you sleeping here alone with some pervert out there who might want to hurt you."

"Gina is just downstairs."

"Two vulnerable women is not better than one."

I flapped my hands around. "I have Harvey. The head detective of the Abingdon police force thought that was plenty! I appreciate that you're worried, but I'm not going to leave Gina in the building alone."

"You're really going to fight me on this? Fine. This is what I get for not having children and not learning how to properly guilt people into doing what I want."

"I think you're doing just fine in that department," I muttered.

She was dialing her phone.

"What are you doing?" I asked.

"Option number two. Calling Maxine. Her husband is the CEO of a security company."

"Becca! What?"

But she was already talking to Maxine. And then to Maxine's husband. And ordering a security guard to sit inside my store every night from closing to opening. Indefinitely.

I sat there listening with my mouth open.

"Please make sure it's one of your best guys. Experienced. Big. Brawny. And we need him armed with more than a nightstick. Something lethal. There's a murderer on the loose. Yes, I'll meet him at the alley entrance in three hours," she said and hung up. "There. Now I'm going home to pack a bag, so make a place for me to sleep while I'm gone."

My lips flapped like a fish's. "You... I... "

But she had already left.

Chapter Eight

BECCA HAD BEEN STAYING at my place for less than twenty-four hours, and already she was driving me nuts. She'd turned up her nose at the idea of sleeping on my aging sofa, claiming it smelled of dog BO. So she opted to share my queen-sized bed with me. In Harvey's spot. So he had to sleep on the floor.

And she snored. Loudly.

She insisted that to prevent wrinkles she had to sleep on her back. Nothing, not even a few desperate shoves in the middle of the night, would dissuade her from the idea.

Honestly, I thought I'd left noisy bedpartners in my past forever.

Then there were her makeup cases and the amount of time she spent in the bathroom endlessly grooming herself. Her bedtime routine alone took over an hour. She scrubbed her face with at least five different things and then layered on ten more. I didn't even ask. It was just a row of assorted serums and lotions that promised all kinds of outlandish things. Sometimes it seemed strange that we'd come from the same DNA pool.

I didn't know who she was doing all this for. She had

boyfriends from time to time, but had never married and said she never intended to. So why was looking young and perfect so important?

The security guard did give me some peace of mind. I tried to cajole Becca into giving me the bill, but she refused. So I tried to repay her kindness by being as nice as possible.

And giving her as much space as I could.

My day hadn't been fun. All anyone wanted to talk about was the murder. Since the scene from the day before was still playing out behind my eyes, I wasn't eager to talk about it, or be constantly reminded of it.

As Glenn had requested, I'd gone through my database and compiled a list of people who'd bought that particular pink yarn in the last year, then walked it down to the police station. Then they fingerprinted me. Glenn reminded me that it was just to eliminate my fingerprints from any others their forensic work might reveal, but it was still a humbling experience.

Despite me scrubbing my fingertips repeatedly, they were stained afterward, and I felt self-conscious about it. I was worried about what my customers would think, so I spent the rest of the day in my office hiding. I didn't want anyone to get the mistaken impression that I might be the murderer.

I normally closed up the shop at six o'clock, but that night a knitting club was using the space after closing. I sent the rest of my staff home and kept myself busy while the group knitted and chatted. Normally I joined them, but I begged off, citing paperwork. They'd planned to stay for a couple of hours, but by 7:15 the members decided to go get a bite to eat and have some drinks and I gratefully closed down the shop completely. Then Harvey and I took off for a long walk to blow off some steam.

The weather had given us a small reprieve. The early signs of spring were getting stronger. As we ambled along I noticed the occasional daffodil or forsythia and their cheerful colors made me feel a little better.

Abingdon is my hometown. It's the right sized city for me. Not too big and not too small. The university brings a lot of culture and the arts to town and I like recognizing many of the faces I see every day. Becca obviously agreed because when her Cedar-Rapids-based bank offered her a choice of branches to manage, she chose Abingdon and moved back home.

When my kids were little it had been wonderful having her so close. But now I was looking for some distance from the toxic interactions that living together for the last twenty-four hours in a one-bedroom apartment had brought on.

Harvey trotted happily at my side, sniffing everything we passed. Occasionally I had to tug a bit to keep him moving as some particularly enticing smell caught his attention and held it. We walked up the historic Seventh Street hill, where some of the houses dated back to the mid-1800s. I loved looking at the intricate architecture. Closer to downtown, these houses had mostly been remodeled or restored. A few of the owners seemed to be in competition over who could make their painted ladies stand out the most, with bright and eye-catching color combinations on all the gingerbread decorations. Others were uniform dark brick, with gleaming white trim and tall columns. A few of these homes were considered mansions and occasionally offered tours to the public.

As we got farther up the hill, and my calves started to protest, the prettier homes gave way to houses of a similar age that hadn't received as much loving care over the years. It seemed like a lot of these had been carved up into rentals for students. The sidewalks had been completely ignored, and I had to watch my step so I didn't trip over cement sections heaved up by invasive tree roots over time.

Harvey got really interested in the trunk of an enormous tree, and I paused for a moment, hoping he'd do his business. I thought maybe we'd come far enough and it was time to head back toward downtown. The tree had never been limbed up properly, and even short little old me had to duck under its branches, which were already leafing out and drooping into the street.

I heard a car door shut and leaned to the side around a branch and a parked car to see who was out there. I was surprised that it was Vincent. But then, it made sense that he'd live in this neighborhood. It was bordering on the fancy houses, and there were probably a lot of affordable fixer-uppers on this end of the street.

I was about to call out a greeting when I realized he was acting furtively. He kept glancing around and then digging through things in the back seat of his car. Apparently he didn't see me or Harvey in the shadow of the tree in the failing light between two parked cars, and Harvey was too preoccupied with the calling cards left by other dogs to notice Vincent. The sound of his sniffing must not have carried that far, because Vincent never looked my way.

Something made me stand and watch silently. I was practically holding my breath to see what he would do. I frowned. My sister's comments from the night before were ringing in my ears. Could Vincent be Mike's killer?

His blank face the day before while I performed CPR flashed in my head. Had he even been surprised to see Mike there? Had he orchestrated the whole thing, using yarn from my store to frame me and shift suspicion away from himself? What if that one clue was the only significant thing the police had to go on? What if he was the murderer, and was going to get away with it, and I'd have to look at him and wonder every morning when he delivered his baked goods to my shop?

Suddenly I didn't feel quite so safe. I noticed for the first time that the streetlight on this block was burned out, and a lot of the houses were dark. Maybe a few were even vacant.

A stray thought hit me—would anyone hear me if I screamed? I'd never been fearful walking through Abingdon, but right then, I felt vulnerable.

I shivered, suddenly a lot colder than I'd felt before.

Gina had been right—the murderer was probably someone we knew. What if it *was* Vincent? Just because I didn't want to believe it was true didn't make it impossible. Even good people could be driven to do terrible things. Wasn't that on the news every single day?

As I watched, Vincent hefted a dark duffel bag over his shoulder, looked around again, missed us, and took off at a brisk pace down an alley on the other side of the street. He disappeared behind some overgrown bushes.

Harvey had made a deposit while I was watching Vincent. I pulled a bag from my pocket and picked up his offering to the doggie smell gods, wrinkling my nose. I tied off the bag and, on impulse, crossed the street. I peered beyond the bushes. I couldn't see Vincent anymore. Where could he have gone? I tried to think what would be on this corresponding section of Eighth Street, but that was a short street, I thought, and ended in a cul-de-sac. In a lifetime lived in this city, I'd never noticed this alley before and had no idea how or where it connected. The shrubs on either side were overgrown, but a single car could pass through there.

I checked my phone. It was still fairly early, only 7:35 p.m. While there were long shadows, it wasn't full dark just yet.

Now I felt like I needed to know where this secret alley went, where Vincent had gone. Was it actually a long lane leading to a house set far back from the street? Maybe a coach house for one of these larger homes? What could his purpose be?

Could he be hiding evidence?

Before I put my phone back in my coat pocket, I dialed my sister's number, but didn't press the call button. If I got myself in a pinch, I could always call her quickly. She was only two to three minutes away by car.

I took a few steps toward the bushes, listening for footfalls. I didn't hear any. Vincent had been moving fast. He was probably long gone. I moved past the bushes gingerly, staying in the shadows. They shed big drops of water on us from the rain the day before.

Past the bushes, the alley had gone to the weeds. The buildings on either side loomed over us, three stories each, large and solid. It was much darker here. I waited a moment while my eyes adjusted to the lower light. I chewed on my lip and thought about what I was doing.

The alley made a right turn at the edge of the property of the house on my right side. There was a large dumpster situated on that corner, overloaded with demolition materials, so that house must have been under renovation. Next to the dumpster was a run-down two-car garage painted in peeling white and dark green paint, that obstructed my view of the alley.

I chucked Harvey's smelly bag in the dumpster, grateful to find a place to be rid of it, and took a few more steps. I'd just go look around that corner and see what was there. An alley was public property like a street, wasn't it? I had every right to use it.

Behind the garage, the alley had been mowed, at least. Back there, the property lines seemed to be indistinct, and the steepness of the hill must have made it difficult to maintain, because there were a lot of trees and overgrown areas on either side. Would that be a good place to dispose of something incriminating? Like a ball of yarn that would decompose within the underbrush where no one would ever look?

I saw a back-porch lamp off to my right and kept going, drawn to its comforting light. I could hear some children playing in one of the yards, and that gave the alley some life and made it feel more normal and safe.

It felt almost rural back there, like a country lane. It was hard to believe this was in the middle of my small city. Vincent was nowhere in sight. I glanced curiously at the backsides of the houses I passed, wondering if one of them had been Vincent's destination. And if so, why had he taken such an indirect route?

This was all so odd.

I switched on the flashlight attached to Harvey's leash and kept walking. I felt a little sheepish. I didn't know what I was doing, exactly. I was being far too nosy, far too suspicious. But my doubts didn't stop me from moving forward at a brisk pace. I guess I thought I might catch up to Vincent and see where he was going.

Harvey was oblivious. He loved having new things to sniff. The plume of his tail swayed over his back as he pranced from weed to fencepost to trash can, his sniffer going ninety miles per hour. I was glad to have his company.

I seemed to walk for a really long time, the yards and even the alley itself getting tidier until it seemed more typical of Abingdon. It dumped us out on Ninth Street, having skipped Eighth altogether. I peeked around judiciously. Vincent was nowhere in sight. I'd never caught up to him, which probably meant he'd never stopped to dispose of anything.

I was both disappointed and relieved.

The houses on Ninth are large, but not quite as grand as the houses on Seventh, and very few have driveways or garages. One of Blaine's childhood friends had lived on that street, and I'd dropped him off and picked him up there a great deal over the years. It was comforting to be on familiar territory again.

Ninth was narrow, with very little clearance between the house fronts and the street itself. You were only supposed to park only on one side, and when people didn't follow that rule, cars had to pull over because two couldn't pass. Finding a parking spot on this street could be tough. Maybe that was why Vincent had parked on Seventh. Perhaps he'd been headed to a dinner party on this street and knew parking would be difficult. That seemed like a logical conclusion and not nefarious at all. I felt a little silly.

Now that I had my bearings, I looked around. Ah, yes. To my right was the infamous local homeless shelter. Run for years and years by a little old lady named Miss Ida, it occasionally was mentioned in the local paper when neighbors complained about it for various reasons. Noise or trash or too many idle people hanging around—whatever excuse they could come up with to try to stop her good work because they were afraid of people down on their luck. Though the paper regularly noted Miss Ida's success stories as well. She helped people find jobs and get back on their feet. Everyone knew Miss Ida.

A handmade sign on the front porch said: "Come in for a Hot Meal and a Warm Bed." All the windows in the large Victorian home glowed yellow-orange behind drawn curtains, and I could smell something cooking. Pot roast, I thought.

My stomach growled. Becca would probably have a salad waiting for me, but I was thinking about the leftover chicken korma in the fridge.

I took one last look around and shrugged uneasily in my warm winter coat. There was no trace of Vincent anywhere that I could see. And while I could explain away the reasons why Vincent might park on Seventh, I couldn't let go of the odd sensation left behind by watching him act so furtively.

It made me feel like I didn't know him at all. Like he could be capable of something scary. It filled me with dread. My whole world had turned upside down. Nothing was what it seemed anymore. A person I knew and trusted had a secret, and with Mike's murder just the day before, my mind was running to uncomfortable places. I had to think of a way to find out more about Vincent's strange foray, and I had to be smart about it so I didn't put myself in danger—if for no other reason than to put my mind at ease about the person I thought of as a friend.

Reluctantly, I turned and headed down the hill for home, with Harvey trotting alongside.

Chapter Nine

GINA WAS LOCKING the door to her apartment as I was heading back downstairs early the next morning. She bent over her phone with a scowl on her face.

"Everything okay?" I asked as we met on her landing.

She held her phone up to show me. "Jacob texted me seventeen times in the middle of the night last night. Seventeen!"

"I thought you broke up?" I said.

She scrolled and tapped at her phone. "Yeah. Over a month ago. He won't stop. I swear he's stalking me."

My brow drew together. "Do you really think that? Should you go talk to campus police?"

She sighed. "No. Maybe. I don't know. I think it'll pass. He's harmless. His super power is being annoying. I guess he's worried because of what happened with Mike. He'd cooled off quite a bit before, but that just revved him up all over again. I'm going to rip him a new one. My snark is his kryptonite." She snarled a bit there at the end and I didn't envy Jacob. At all.

"If there's any doubt, you should go to the police. It's—"

"Better to be safe than sorry? I know. I'll take care of it. If I feel threatened at all, I'll go to campus police." She arched a brow and made a point to look up toward the third floor. "How's the perpetual pajama party upstairs going?"

I sighed dramatically and headed down the last flight. I wondered if Gina had heard me yelling at Becca the night before to hurry up in the bathroom because I needed to use it. I probably should have gone down to the shop and used the public restroom instead, but I'd been tired and wanted to sleep, and she'd already been in there for over an hour.

Gina hustled down after me. "That bad? Spill the tea, lady."

"She means well," I murmured. She was just so fussy. I wondered how long she was going to keep this up before she just went home. She kept complaining that she didn't have access to her full stash of cosmetics. And that my apartment was too small. And that Harvey's fur was getting on her clothes. So far, her love for me was winning out over her love of thirty-seven shades of blush to choose from. For now.

Gina went into the shop and started our opening procedures. Trevor, the security guard, came to stand in the doorway of my office as I checked over my calendar. My paper calendar. Which I'd be lost without. He had his uniform ball cap in his hand and scratched at his hair, then stooped to ruffle Harvey's fur. "Another quiet night," he commented.

"That's a relief," I replied. And it was. No late-night shenanigans next door. No surprises in the alley. Now if I could just get Becca to stop worrying and go home, I'd get a good night's sleep. As it was I'd had to rearrange my schedule and get up even earlier so she had a full two hours to get ready for work—after listening to her snore like a rabid chainsaw all night.

Trevor waved his cap at me and set it back on his head. "See you tonight."

"See you."

I was tying on my apron when Vincent came in with our pastry delivery. He seemed the same as every other day. We exchanged our normal pleasantries. When he was about to leave, I handed him a coffee and watched him carefully through my lashes as I pretended to wipe down the counter. I kept my voice just as light and lively as it had been all along. I didn't want him to know that I was feeling suspicious. Or nosy. Well, too nosy. "I was walking Harvey up Seventh last night and I thought I saw you, but I wasn't sure. Do you live on Seventh?"

Vincent went still. His normally animated face lost all expression. He looked like an entirely different person.

I forgot to breathe as I watched this sudden transformation.

"No," he said gruffly. "It wasn't me."

"Oh, sorry," I forced myself to reply breezily. "Mistaken identity. It was getting dark and I didn't get a good look." I pushed a smile onto my lips and hoped it looked genuine.

He narrowed his eyes at me, turned, and left.

My smile fell. Trepidation settled over me as I stared through the window at the spot where he'd disappeared from sight, marching stiffly back to his store.

Vincent had just lied to me. About something as inconsequential as parking on a street.

Could Becca be right about him? Suddenly I felt deeply and profoundly sad.

"That was weird," Gina commented, coming to stand next to me at the counter. "I've never seen him act so rude."

"Yeah," I replied. "Especially since I'm sure it was him."

She looked at me with wide eyes. "Weirder."

The bell over the door tinkled and Marilyn swept in. She slammed her purse down on the counter and patted her hair, making sure it was still in place. "Whew. I just about bit it out there. Mr. Pradel must have a dark cloud over his shoulder.

The man almost knocked me down. I guess he didn't see me."

Gina and I exchanged glances, her lips twisting off to one side. "Extra weird," she whispered in my direction, and then she jogged around the counter and ushered Marilyn to her favorite spot, making sure she was okay, while I whipped up her favorite coffee.

The day was much like any other, with the same natural ebb and flow, but there was a pall on everything I said and did, what everyone around me said and did. My heart felt heavy and my thoughts were dark as I went through the motions of my routine with a smile plastered on my face.

The gossip was all about Mike Blankenship and who might have wanted to murder him. I made a point of pulling aside all of my employees and reminding them not to participate in *any* of the gossip while they were working.

It was impossible not to listen to it, though. Every customer had a theory, and they all seemed to stem from Mike's lewd attempts at a love life. There were more than a few young women he'd used and ghosted. And several stories of young men who'd had their girlfriends poached, as though women were a resource men competed for instead of individuals in control of their own lives. I cringed to hear people talk about young women that way.

Those were horrible, awful things, but were they a motive for murder? I supposed that anything could be a motive for murder if someone got angry enough. But how would the police narrow it down to one individual when Mike had injured so many?

I was sitting and chatting with Marilyn when Ben Davies came in, looking utterly miserable. Poor kid. He got a coffee and a pastry and sat at a table by himself in the back corner of the store, hunched over, unmoving. I rose. "Excuse me, Marilyn, for just a moment."

My fingers itched to squeeze his shoulder or his arm as I glided by him, but I didn't do that. I just perched on the chair opposite him so he'd know I wouldn't stay if I found I wasn't welcome. Ben and I had developed a bit of a rapport when he'd been shopping for his girlfriend a few months before, but I didn't know if that still had meaning for him. "How are you holding up, Ben?" I asked gently.

He tried to smile at me, but his face crumpled. He rubbed his face with his hands, as though he could wipe away the grief, and didn't make direct eye contact with me. "I don't know what to do with myself anymore," he choked out, clearly trying really hard not to cry.

It didn't seem like he wanted me to go away, so I settled into the seat more firmly. My hands fluttered around. I wanted to soothe him somehow, but didn't feel like I knew him well enough for that. "What do you mean?"

"It's just... I used to go sit... next door... for an hour or two every afternoon before I started my shift. We'd have some laughs. Play some video games. Maybe watch Mike do some ink. Now I just... I don't know."

I frowned and nodded.

"My life is crap," he blurted out. "I've got a degree from EIU and I'm just working in a factory. My mom keeps going on and on about my potential and how I need to apply myself. And she's right. I've just been goofing off for years. I'm so tired of being poor and not doing anything with my life. I used to think I was going to be somebody."

I patted his hand twice. He wasn't even thirty yet, but I understood the angst. I'd been a young mother and stayed home with my children right after college. While that had been an important and fulfilling job, the day to day monotony had chipped away at my feelings of self-worth.

I was surprised he was opening up to me, but I'd had plenty of practice momming my own boys and their friends.

"You're young. You can still do whatever you want. I opened this store in my forties. You've got plenty of time."

Ben dashed at his eyes. "But shit happens so fast. Mike's just… gone."

I didn't know what to say to that. I looked at him with sympathy.

Ben studied his pastry intensely. "We had a fight a couple weeks ago and hadn't spoken since. Everything's just… It's messed up. I had stopped drinking a few months earlier, trying to get back on track. Lauren quit too, and I've been encouraging her to paint again. She used to be so good, you know. Her professors thought she could make it as an artist. I don't know. It seems like she's given up. And… I have too. I got sick during college—really sick. It threw everything off and I just— I never bounced back. Nothing is working the way it was supposed to. My whole life is blown. I can't fix it. And I can't stop being mad at him. And… I still… miss him." He grimaced and shook his head. "Don't worry. The police know about the fight. I'm a suspect, apparently, and I don't even have an alibi."

"You too?"

He looked shocked. "You? Charlie? That's savage. Why are you a suspect?"

"Same reason as you, I suppose." I remembered what Glenn Swinarski had said about not repeating the detail about the yarn. I'd told Becca because I knew she wouldn't repeat it, but I wouldn't tell another soul. However, I thought it was harmless to tell him I was a suspect too, and hoped it might make him feel less stressed about the situation. It sounded like he had enough on his plate with his grief alone. Mike Blankenship must have had some redeeming qualities if his friends were this distressed over his loss. And somehow I knew Ben wasn't the person who'd killed him. He'd always seemed so genuine and kind and down-to-earth, apologetic when his friends had done wrong. He'd never had anything to gain by that. I couldn't imagine this sweet young man in front of me taking a life.

It changed things for me, a little, in my head. Some of the gladness for the peace that Mike's absence had brought ebbed away, and I felt a little ashamed of myself. Somewhere in Abingdon Mike's parents, sister, and other family members were grieving his loss too.

I was thinking about that and patting Ben's hand again when I said, "Follow your dreams, Ben. Wherever they lead you."

He looked like he was suffocating. "I don't have any."

I squeezed his hand instinctively. "I know what that feels like. When I was a stay-at-home mom I felt like, is this it? Is this all there is? Is this my only contribution to the world? Then I took some part-time jobs in coffee shops and my whole world expanded. Those jobs forced me to be more social, to start living more vibrantly. Then I started knitting as a hobby. I was good at it and it made me so happy. I found myself dreaming about a place I could make that would be like a second home for people like me. You don't have to bust out of the womb knowing what you'll do with your life. Very few people do. There must be something you enjoy, some aptitude that you have already or maybe haven't even discovered yet. That will be the thing that drives you. Just don't focus on the money—focus on being happy. The rest will come."

There seemed to be a little hope rising in him. His eyes wandered back and forth as he thought about what I was saying. "There might be some things I can try."

"That's the spirit." I beamed and squeezed his hand again.

Someone slow clapped behind me. "Inspirational. Do you charge by the hour?"

I turned. It was Lauren, her eyes flashing.

Ben straightened in his chair and scooted it back with a loud squeal. "Lauren!"

I pulled my hands back toward myself and blinked, looking for an escape route. Except there wasn't one. Lauren was blocking the only way out of my seat.

Lauren's cheek twitched with anger as she looked down at me. "Don't you think you're a bit old for him? You could be his mother."

I think my brows went straight up to my hairline. "I was just—"

"Yeah. You were just," she spat.

Ben's voice was like gravel and his nostrils flared. He was clearly angry. "Cut it out, Lauren. She's just trying to help me. And you've got no room to talk about anything like that and you know it."

Lauren's face went bright red. She whispered with venom, "Don't you dare."

I squirmed in my seat. I felt like I was intruding on something very personal.

"Why aren't you at work?" he asked tiredly.

"I had some openings between clients and I thought I'd see how you were doing. Andrea told me you were here. She just didn't tell me you were looking for other women to comfort you."

He barely moved his mouth. "That's enough. I'm leaving." To me he said, "I'm sorry, Charlie. We're all under a lot of stress right now. Thank you for talking to me." Then he stalked off, leaving his coffee and pastry on the table. Lauren immediately took off after him. She chased him across the street and out of view down the block.

I got up, thinking I'd go hide in my office for a few minutes and try to knit away the stress Lauren had just dumped on me, but I noticed Marilyn was gathering up her things. I felt I should go say goodbye to her first. Maybe just a few more minutes with her would calm me down. I settled into the chair opposite her, still a little shell-shocked.

Marilyn slid me a side eye. "Well, that was something."

I squinched my eyes. "You heard?"

"Honey, everybody heard. It's not a big store. That young lady has some issues. Don't pay her any attention. You were doing the Lord's work for that boy."

"Sometimes I feel like a priest." I chuckled. "Everyone tells me their troubles."

Marilyn had all her things gathered together and set her purse and her knitting bag on her lap. "That's just because you're a wonderful person and easy to talk to."

I smiled. "You going to see your granddaughter today?"

"I am. After my nail appointment. The poor girl. She's in so much pain and no one seems to know why. She's missed so much school and seen so many doctors."

"I'm sorry to hear she's not better," I said. "I hope the doctors find something soon."

"And I'm glad to hear Lauren Waters won't be at Phalanges while I'm getting my nails done. Bless me, Father, for I have sinned." She smiled wickedly. "I'm sorry. I shouldn't gossip. But that young lady's always stirring up some kind of trouble."

"Oh?"

"Oh, yes. She can make a set of stunning nails. Most amazing nail art you ever saw. Might as well be in a magazine. Probably has a million followers on Instagram. But it doesn't last more than a couple hours before it pops off. Did mine once. Stunning. But I had to have it redone the next day. Nobody's got time for that. I don't know why they keep her on. There's always someone in there complaining about her work. The girl I see now doesn't do anything fancy. It's basic. But it lasts."

I looked at my own nails. They were bare. I clipped them

regularly so they wouldn't get in my way. That was all I had ever done. Then I looked at Marilyn's. They were done with a glossy purple polish. They'd obviously grown a bit, because I could see her natural nail peeking out by the cuticle, but there wasn't a chip in sight. "Well, yours are always lovely. Maybe I should try it sometime."

"Just ask for anyone at Phalanges—except Lauren Waters —and you'll be happy."

"Good to know."

Chapter Ten

AT 7:20 P.M. I found myself dressed in dark colors and headed toward that same dense tree on Seventh Street, with a pocket full of Harvey's favorite treats in case I needed to distract him to keep him quiet. I'd even taken the precaution of putting washi tape over Harvey's tags so they wouldn't jingle. I was going in on full stealth mode.

Maybe I watched too much TV for my own good.

The rain was back, and we were experiencing a cold snap so it was starting to freeze. My winter coat protected me from the worst of it, but my legs and feet were really feeling it. At least the rain clouds made it darker than the day before, which would conceal us better. I hoped. I had to assume my questions that morning would make Vincent even more paranoid.

To my delight there was an ancient SUV parked right next to the tree, granting me more solid cover. It was a dark color, had tinted windows, and was taller than me. So much the better. I didn't even have to crouch down to hide myself.

We staked out our spot and Harvey was happily sniffing the tree again. There was no sign of Vincent so far.

The thick foliage kept most of the freezing rain off me, but every now and then the wind kicked up and a bunch of big drops were dislodged from the branches overhead, landing on my thick, wool hat and coat with a staccato splatter, startling me, and making me reconsider this endeavor.

I was feeling nervous and frankly pretty foolish. I was well aware that I was acting like a nosy neighbor and was hoping I wouldn't catch a cold as a result of this dubious outing. But my curiosity was sky high and I couldn't *not* go. A little bit of paranoia wasn't necessarily a bad thing, especially considering there'd just been a murder in my back alley.

If Vincent showed up tonight, I was going to find out what he was up to. I wasn't sure how his mysterious actions might relate to Mike Blankenship's murder, but he'd lied to me less than forty-eight hours after the murder had occurred and was acting suspicious. It could be important, though it wasn't anything strong enough to share with the police. Not yet. I didn't want to be one of *those* people.

But there was no harm in taking a walk with my dog in the rain—with a bright pink can of pepper spray in my coat pocket that I'd filched from my sister's purse. I wasn't stupid.

I kept checking the time on my phone, which required a ridiculous amount of fumbling around because I was afraid of getting my phone wet. My fingers were stiff and tingling with the cold as I popped one of them out of its mitten to press the home button. I was feeling pretty ridiculous just standing there in one spot, and hoped no one had noticed me.

It would be rich indeed if someone called the cops on *me*.

By 7:35 Harvey was sitting back on his haunches watching me. I occasionally flipped a treat his way to keep his attention on me, since he'd had enough of the sniffing. I'd always wondered how long he would smell something if he was given free rein. Now I knew. Nine and a half minutes was enough time to smell a tree trunk fully saturated by the dogs that travelled up and down Seventh Street.

At least I'd learned *something* from my first-ever surveillance mission.

I was beginning to think Vincent wasn't coming. Maybe it wasn't a regular thing. Maybe it was something he'd done once and that was it.

At 7:43 p.m. a car pulled up on the other side of the street. A door slammed. Harvey started toward the back of the SUV, but I redirected him with a treat and he refocused on me.

I peered sideways through the tinted windows. It was Vincent. And he was doing the same things he'd done the day before. I stayed where I was, using my peripheral vision to watch for movement while staying as still as possible.

When he headed down the alley, I peeked around the back end of the SUV and saw him take one last look before disappearing through the bushes. Yep. Confirmed. It wasn't my imagination. He was acting suspicious as all get-out. Something was definitely not right about this situation. I was going to feel pretty awful if it had nothing to do with Mike Blankenship, but I was willing to take that risk.

I jogged across the street. Carefully. I'm in my early fifties, live on the third floor, and am on my feet all day. I can't afford slipping and falling and breaking a leg. Or, heaven forbid, a hip.

I stayed in the shadow of the house on the right as I approached the bushes, then cautiously looked around them. He was disappearing around the garage in the back. As soon as he rounded the corner, I took off after him, attempting to match his pace without making any noise. I figured the rain was masking most of the sound. It was all I could hear except for the occasional car traveling down Seventh.

When Vincent slipped out of sight into the tree-lined alley, I left the shelter of the garage.

No porch lights were lit. No children played in the back yards. It was darker and creepier than the night before. The

trees looked so grey and ominous they reminded me of dark
fairy tales meant to warn children off of doing foolish things.
Things like this. My pulse was drumming in my head. This was
crazy. I was stalking an acquaintance on a wild hunch. I was a
crazy stalker lady.

And I was freezing. My. Booty. Off.

The wind kept throwing the ice at me sideways so it pelted
my face and cut right through my heavy winter coat.

I considered going back. Briefly. But a little voice in my
head kept saying I might find out something important that
could solve the murder. Acting like a busybody was a small
price to pay. Even if I had to be embarrassed at the end of this.

Staying hidden got a little dicier as the route became more
like a typical alley on the approach to Ninth. But by that point,
he'd long since stopped looking around. I stayed as far back as
I dared. I didn't want to lose him again and have this whole
miserable thing be a waste of my time.

I began to think about my endgame. Or... the lack of it.
Would I confront him directly? Or keep spying? I guessed that
would depend on what he did next. I'd have to wing it. But I
wasn't sure I could stay outside much longer without risking
frostbite. I was dressed very warmly, like a good northern
Midwesterner, but I could barely feel my feet and I'd stumbled
a few times on ruts in the lane and slipped a bit on the ice that
was building up quickly.

Vincent got to Ninth Street and I saw him go off to the
right. I urged my old body forward as fast as I could go,
charging out of the alley huffing like a locomotive. To my right,
I heard a creaky storm door slam shut. I looked up and down
the street. Not a soul was outside.

I replayed the sound of the door shutting in my mind, now
that I wasn't distracted by racing after Vincent. The sound had
been close. Real close. And he was gone. He had to have gone
into one of the nearest homes on the right side of the alley.

Could he have gone into Miss Ida's shelter? Was Vincent homeless? Could he have lost his home and managed to hold onto his business?

My heart squeezed painfully. That would explain all of his behavior, wouldn't it? Every last bit.

I chewed my lip indecisively. How far was I going to take this? Would I embarrass this perfectly nice man when he was struggling?

No.

I would not do that.

I turned to walk down the hill on Ninth feeling like an absolute fool. I'd jumped to conclusions and gone on a wild-goose chase. I was a silly old lady with nothing better to do than peek through the curtains at my neighbors. I frowned deeply and began reconsidering my life goals.

The sidewalks were getting treacherous and I was already so cold. If only I had a toboggan, I could slide right down the hill practically all the way home, where I could whip up a nice hot cappuccino.

Harvey was fine, of course. Great Pyrenees had been bred for this kind of weather in the mountains of southern France, with a double coat of fluffy white fur. He glanced up at me, his tongue lolling out in a happy smile. It made me smile too, pulling me mostly out of my funk. He was such a good boy. I was paying for my foolishness, but he was having a great time. At least that was something.

"Charlotte?"

I whirled around. Vincent stood on Miss Ida's porch. He looked grim.

I instantly made the decision to play dumb. "Oh! Vincent! Fancy meeting you here. I was just walking Harvey. He loves this kind of weather." I cut myself off before I laid it on too thick. Besides, my teeth were chattering and I could barely form words properly.

He looked like he was assessing me. Then he visibly came to a decision. "Where are my manners? Why don't you come inside and warm up for a minute? I'll make you a warm drink."

"Thank you, but no. Harvey needs to do his business."

"Charlotte, you're shivering and you've got ice dripping from your braid. Come inside a minute before you catch your death. I'll get someone to drive you home."

I bowed my head a moment, thinking about what a horrible person I was. Then I agreed to go inside so I didn't turn into a human icicle.

Miss Ida's home was neat as a pin and so, so, so, so warm. Vincent took my hat, scarf, and coat and hung them on a wooden coat rack beside the door. I stood in the foyer with my hands clenched, unable to think about anything but absorbing all the warmth possible. Vincent bustled off through a closed door to get me something to drink, though I'd urged him not to. I guessed that was the kitchen. I could hear pots and pans rattling around. The house seemed quiet otherwise. I wondered how many other people were staying there at the moment.

I swung my braid over my shoulder and found that it was positively crunchy with ice, now melting slowly, and a sizable shard was hanging from the end. Goodness. That couldn't be good for it. I broke off the shard and then I didn't know what to do with it, so I let it melt in my hand and brushed the wetness off on my pants.

Now that my eyeballs had thawed, I could see that the house had last been decorated a decade or two before the 1960s and 1970s had turned everything into a bright orange and avocado-green nightmare. From the foyer I could see into the formal living room. The door was open and the lights were all on in there. Ivory lace curtains encrusted large swaths of the wall, interrupting the robin's-egg blue paint. The chairs were all dusty rose and dove grey, and the sofa was pale yellow with bright red flowers and dull green leaves.

It was tasteful and traditional, if a bit worn in places, with mementos and tchotchkes lining every surface. It was clear that someone had cared for these furnishings lovingly over the years, and there wasn't a speck of dust in sight. All the wood—floors and tables alike—gleamed with polish. It was heavily scented with the warm, welcoming smells of cleaning agents and the singular odor of the elderly. It felt exceedingly homey to me.

Harvey whined softly, just a faint whistle of a sound, and I glanced down at him. "It's okay, sweet boy," I said, and stroked his soft ears. I knew he was feeling anxious about being somewhere new. I felt bad about bringing a dog into a stranger's home. I hoped he wouldn't leave too much hair behind for Miss Ida or her lodgers to clean up.

I heard the sound of a whisk rapidly striking a metal bowl and wondered what I was going to say to Vincent now. Did he know what I'd been doing? He had to have guessed, but he was being a gentleman anyway.

A staircase with a curving balustrade led to the second floor, and I turned to look at the plethora of pictures in an eclectic montage of frames lining the pale yellow wall next to it. Many were portraits in black and white or sepia and white, some with lips, eyes, and hair lightly colored in. A few had that fuzzy, yellowed look of photos from the 1970s. A handful were modern snapshots. "Oh," I murmured. One was of Vincent, laughing, in a bright purple bow tie and crisp, pale pink shirt.

"Yes, I'm one of Miss Ida's graduates," Vincent said from behind me. He stood in the doorway to the kitchen holding a silver tray. Behind him, I could see an original turquoise vintage kitchen before the door swung shut.

"I didn't know," I said lamely.

"The people on that wall are those she considers her

nonbiological family." He moved into the formal living room and set the tray on the glossy coffee table. "Please, won't you join me?"

"I'm sorry to be so much trouble," I blurted as I perched on one of the grey armchairs and commanded Harvey to lie down next to it. He obeyed, his large brown eyes rolling back and forth between me and Vincent worriedly.

Vincent didn't reply, instead handing me a mug of hot chocolate topped with whipped cream and cinnamon as he sat on the floral sofa. I accepted gratefully, hugging the mug between both hands. It instantly dispelled the remaining cold lingering there and left my fingers tingling.

"Ida is sleeping now, and I'll be here until morning. I stay and keep watch a few nights a week. A few of us take turns so she's never alone and has all the help she needs. Her hearing is all but gone, and we want to keep her safe. She won't allow the doors to be locked. There's only been one troublesome incident in all the years she's been doing this, but she's no longer the spitfire she once was, and… we worry."

"I see. What a wonderful thing to do." I sipped the chocolate. Of course, it was absolutely amazing. Rich. Likely made with straight cream. Insanely decadent, but oh so good. I felt the warmth trickle down, getting into every last cold nook and cranny.

Inwardly, I cringed. I felt like a heel.

"We love her. You'd do the same."

I nodded. Just like my sister was doing for me. My eyes welled up, and I had to make a point of looking up at the ceiling to get control of myself. I hoped my struggle didn't play out all over my face. But it probably did.

It had been a rough week.

His expression softened. "I texted one of our clients. He drives for Uber. He's going to be here in ten minutes to take you home."

"Thank you. That's so kind of you," I said. In my head I was panicking, wondering if I had enough in my wallet for a huge tip. I was also realizing that I didn't deserve his kindness.

"After the last few days, it's the least I can do. We're all a little on edge right now, aren't we?"

I let out a sigh. "I'm seeing potential murderers in every face I look at, it seems." That was as close as I could get to an admission of guilt unless he asked me directly. He was all kinds of polite, so I didn't think he'd put me through that.

He nodded understanding. I think he got it—all of it—the fears that had driven me to follow him and my regret. And now his need for privacy made complete sense. There was a hugely unfair social stigma attached to homelessness. There was no way I was going to ask about the circumstances that had brought him to that state or how he'd worked his way out of it.

He relaxed into the sofa, looking more like his usual self, and I relaxed too. This would probably be a turning point in our relationship. Either we'd be closer on the other side of this or he'd avoid me entirely. I hoped it would bring us closer. I now found I admired and respected him even more.

"I don't suppose you've heard anything from the police chief about suspects?" he asked.

"Aside from myself? No."

He swallowed a sip, and his mouth twisted in a wry smile. "Me too. Twinsies. There are too many people it could be. I don't know how they'll narrow it down."

I frowned. "Me either."

"For the record, the police cleared me. I have multiple witnesses who place me here all night on the night of the murder."

I nodded soberly. If his claim checked out, and I was sure it would, Vincent Pradel would no longer be on my list of possible suspects for Mike Blankenship's murder.

I was back to square one.

Chapter Eleven

I STOOD at the door of my apartment, moving like molasses as I gathered my things. I was up much earlier than usual because I just couldn't sleep anymore. I was thinking about calling in an extra person in the afternoon so I could take a nap. Becca's snoring was making me crazy.

Harvey whined and pawed at the door, then let out a piercing bark. I shushed him. He moved restlessly a few paces and barked again and again. He must have really needed to go. He wasn't normally much of a barker, though most Pyrs, especially females, tended to be, from what I had read.

"What is his problem?" Becca asked, peering around the door leading out of my bedroom with a towel on her head and a sour expression on her face.

"No idea," I replied. Though I actually wondered if he was acting squirrelly because he was as sleep deprived as I was.

When I was finally ready to unlatch the door and pull it open, Harvey bolted out, also very unlike him. He stopped a few steps down the stairs, let out a series of loud, throaty barks, and began to growl.

Great Pyrenees have impressive barks. Painfully loud.

Enough to easily match a Doberman, Rottweiler or German Shepherd in ferocity. He barreled down the rest of the stairs.

I was instantly awake and alert.

That was extremely unusual behavior.

I looked over the banister. The back door was cracked open, and as I came down a few more steps, I realized that the small back room that housed the stairwell—and was where we received inventory—was flooded with crisp, cold air, so it had been like that for a while. There were huge boxes scattered across the floor, some of them upended and crumpled. That was strange. Sometimes inventory built up in there before we could get it all put away, but when we'd closed down the store the night before, we'd zeroed all the new boxes out.

What could have happened there?

"Trevor?" I called as I raced down the stairs.

There was no answer. The security guard should have been there. He never left until we spoke in the morning. He could be in the bathroom, but… that didn't explain Harvey's behavior.

I called Trevor's name again, louder.

Silence.

Harvey danced in a circle among the boxes, barking his head off.

My heart rate picked up and dread settled in my stomach.

Harvey wheeled around and headed into the store, barking even louder, interspersed with desperate plaintive whining. There had only been one other time in his life that he'd whined with that strange note of desperation. The morning I had found Mike Blankenship. A wave of nausea rolled through me. What was I going to find in the store?

"Trevor?"

Please answer. Please answer. Please answer.

Nothing.

I stepped slowly toward the store. It was dark. I couldn't see a thing.

"Charlie?" Gina called down the stairwell.

"Something's wrong," I yelled back. There was no point in being quiet. I'd already been yelling. Harvey had been barking. If there was someone in the store, they already knew I was there. "Get your phone and call the police!"

I dearly wished I had my sister's pepper spray in my hand. I almost yelled to Gina to go into my apartment to get it, but I was afraid to. Afraid of what might happen if I did. That it might make a desperate person do something terrible. But it was a catch-22. Not having something defensive also made me vulnerable.

I felt almost certain that someone was in the store.

Gina ran down the stairs behind me. I glanced back. She was still in PJs and hadn't brushed her hair yet. I waved at her to stay back, out of sight.

I heard a loud thump coming from the store, like something hitting a wall. Hard.

Adrenaline pumped through me.

Harvey could be in danger. What if there was someone in there with a gun?

The paralysis of my fear broke. Harvey was my everything. I couldn't let someone hurt him.

I strode into the store and slapped on every single light at once, hoping to stun anyone there whose eyes might be adjusted to the dark and give me a second to figure out what to do. The store was empty. And there was a decrepit old moving dolly leaning up against the wall on the outside of my office that we had not left there.

My office. That was where Harvey was. I could hear him whining and his paws scrabbling on the tile flooring. The light was already on in there. Its switch was over by all the others because the building was so old.

I was there in three steps.

I didn't scream. That would have wasted too much precious time. I flew into action.

Trevor was trussed up in my desk chair the same way Mike Blankenship had been in the alley. But he was still moving, kind of flapping his hands at the ends of his restraints and drumming his feet against the chair base like he was almost out of the energy needed to fight. The thump I'd heard was him banging the chair into the wall to get my attention.

My ancient desk drawer was already open, and my expensive Swiss stainless-steel scissors lay on top of my other stationery supplies as though someone had discarded them there in a hurry. I grabbed them and held Trevor's head steady against my chest as I slit the blue plastic shopping bag open with a calm precision I didn't know I had in me. I pulled the pieces away from his face and bent to work on the pink yarn around his neck. It was wrapped really tightly and was clearly compromising his airway. Oddly, I noted a few of the strands had already been cut.

Had the murderer changed their mind?

Trevor was breathing again, but it was more like a wheeze being dragged through a collapsed straw. He wasn't getting enough air. His face was bright red and his eyes were bulging. There were so many layers of yarn I had to slip the scissors under the strands repeatedly with care so I didn't cut his throat. Luckily they're very sharp scissors. I worked as fast as I could.

Finally I got them cut free.

Trevor's head rocked against the back of the chair. He rasped in deep breaths, then coughed and gagged, his chest heaving and spittle flying around his face.

I started cutting the rest of the yarn restraining him—first the yarn around his chest, so he could get as deep a breath as he wanted, then his arms on the armrests and his ankles tied to the center spindle of the rolling desk chair.

I had to push Harvey away a few times. He was anxiously whining and pawing at Trevor and I didn't want his nails to scratch the man. Trevor needed some room to breathe and get his composure back.

Behind me in the store I heard Gina talking on her phone, on speaker, to a police dispatcher.

"He's breathing now," she said, her voice breathy and a little higher than usual. "Charlie got him free."

"There's a unit on the way. And an ambulance. Can you let them in when they get there?" the dispatcher asked.

"Yes, I'll let them in. Are they coming to the front or to the alleyway?" Leave it to Gina to think of everything when I'd have just told them to hurry.

"Let me check," the dispatcher said.

I tuned out their conversation and refocused on Trevor. He'd doubled over, bracing his elbows on his knees with his hands cupping his face, still breathing hard. He hadn't said a word yet.

I pushed Harvey back again and gave him the command "down," in my no-nonsense voice, pointing at his bed.

He reluctantly lay down but didn't lower his head and didn't stop whining, soft and low. He wriggled forward by millimeters, trying to get to Trevor and trying to obey my command. He was distressed but he'd be okay. I'd reward him later. Without Harvey's guarding instinct kicking in, I might have been a few minutes slower to find Trevor, and that could have cost him his life. But for now he needed to be a good boy and stay out of the way.

I put my hand on Trevor's back, like I'd done so many times when my own boys had been hurt or sad. "An ambulance is on the way," I said.

"Okay. That was close." His voice was raspy and harsh and he was still taking deep breaths. He looked at Harvey, his eyes wide and glossy. "I think your dog just saved my life. Can I—can I thank him?"

"Of course."

Trevor opened his arms. Harvey rose up on his front paws and looked back and forth between me and Trevor. I said, "Okay," to release him from his command. He leapt up and went straight into Trevor's embrace, snuffling him all over while Trevor shuddered and started to cry, petting him and thanking him over and over again.

I sniffed and looked over at Gina through the doorway. She was watching, her face pale and tracked with tears.

The police arrived a few minutes later, with the paramedics just a minute or two behind them, along with a fire truck. The front of the store was alight with flashing red-and-blue emergency lights in the predawn. Becca had come down to see what all the commotion was about. She lingered in the back room by the stairs, watching, her expression drawn. The officers milled around the store while the paramedics checked Trevor out. The paramedics concluded that Trevor was probably fine but should go to the hospital for a thorough exam as a precaution. I was glad Trevor didn't argue with that. He needed to be checked by a doctor.

Glenn Swinarski strode in just as the paramedics made that announcement. Glenn nodded at me, a flinty expression on his face, and went into my office to talk to Trevor. After a few moments of conferring with Trevor, he turned and beckoned to me. I slipped inside, and Glenn closed the door. It was a tight fit. Trevor remained seated in my office chair while Glenn and I stood.

Glenn said, "Trevor feels he's okay to give me an initial statement, right now, before he goes to the hospital. We'll be following up for more detail after that, but as the owner of the property you need to be here for this. He just told me he hasn't informed you about what happened yet."

I let out a breath. "Okay."

Of course I wanted to know, but I wasn't going to press a man who'd just nearly died, and I'd figured the police would be asking him anyway.

Glenn turned his attention to Trevor.

Trevor spread his hands, which were a little shaky. He looked drained of color and his movements were limp and enervated. "I never got a good look at them and they never said a word. Someone knocked on the back door. I called through the door that the store was closed. They knocked again. Like a fool, I opened it, thinking it was UPS or something. They had a dolly stacked high with big boxes—piled so high I couldn't see the person at all. As soon as I opened the door, they shoved them at me. The boxes were fricking heavy. They fell on me and knocked me down. I guess I blacked out. When I woke up I was in this chair in the dark. They had me mostly tied up. The bag was already over my head, but it was a little bit loose and I was getting some air at that point. I started to fight, you know. Trying to get out of the ties. They pulled the bag down tight around my neck and started wrapping the rope around."

He gingerly fingered his throat, which still had raised red welts encircling it from the tightly wound yarn. "I was already getting woozy, but I clearly heard a dog barking upstairs. I think that spooked them. I heard sounds like they were rummaging around frantically, then I felt something cold on my neck. I thought they were going to cut my throat, but they stopped. They took off, and the next thing I knew Mrs. Shaw's dog was in here whining and pawing at me, and Mrs. Shaw cut me loose a minute later. Thank God for that dog. I was almost gone. I've never had a dog in my life. Didn't think I liked them." His face had the blank look of disbelief. I think he was in shock. I grabbed an afghan meant for a charity bazaar off a filing cabinet and draped it over him.

"My desk drawer was open and my scissors were lying on top. Someone had definitely gotten them out," I volunteered.

Glenn was nodding. "You say you didn't get a good look at them, but did you get an impression of size, height or weight? Maybe skin or hair color?"

"The bag wasn't exactly easy to see through, and it was pretty dark. The only light was from the streetlight coming through the front windows, and they had the chair turned to face the back wall. They'd turned off the lights I had on here in the office." Trevor stared into space and his eyes roved back and forth. He blew a breath out through tight lips. "I can't tell you anything except they were shorter than the stack of boxes. I'm sorry."

Whoever it was had gotten Trevor into that chair, so they would've had to be strong. Trevor wasn't particularly bulky. He was just an average-sized guy. But I'd have been hard pressed to pick his dead weight up and get him in a chair. Had they maybe used the dolly that they'd left behind in the shop?

Trevor pinched his eyes closed, clearly still trying to remember details. "I can tell you they were wearing gloves."

"Workman's gloves?"

"No, they were like medical gloves. Latex exam gloves." Trevor put his hand to the back of his neck and closed his eyes, breathing deeply.

"I think that's enough for now. You go get checked out," Glenn said to Trevor, patting his shoulder. He turned to me. "I'll need my detectives to go through the place. You won't be able to open for a few hours, if at all today. Was anything disturbed?"

"I didn't touch anything except the scissors to cut him free," I said. The drawer they'd been in was still open, and the stainless-steel scissors gleamed on the surface of the desk. Otherwise, everything's as it was."

"Stay close so you can answer questions. And check to

make sure nothing's missing. You did good here, Charlotte. Your quick thinking saved his life."

"I only wish I'd gotten there in time for Mike Blankenship," I said sadly.

I followed Glenn out of my office and into the tiny back room. He stood there staring at the boxes scattered around the floor while the paramedics got Trevor on a stretcher to take him to the hospital. I could smell coffee brewing. Gina would be making some for the officers. Becca had disappeared, probably gone upstairs to finish getting ready for work. She wouldn't want to be seen *en dishabille*.

"You have a box cutter handy?" Glenn asked, pulling on a pair of gloves like the ones Trevor had just described.

I produced a box cutter from a shelf nearby and handed it to him. I had several in strategic places for opening up new inventory.

He slid the blade out and bent over the nearest box. "Let's see what's in these."

Glenn sliced it open with deft cuts and flipped up the flaps. "Books," he said. "Old ones."

I leaned over. They looked like a mix of ancient encyclopedias and other old, musty hardcover books. Library smells tickled my nose. "If all the boxes are filled with books, that explains how they knocked Trevor out. Each box would have to weigh fifty pounds or more."

"At least. Probably closer to a hundred. That'd be a lot for one person to manage." He carefully slit open each box, but didn't touch the contents, revealing more of the same. There were seven large boxes in total. "They better check him for a concussion."

I murmured agreement. It was staggering to think about. "The whole thing was carefully planned," I remarked. "It makes me wonder if more than one person was involved."

He looked thoughtful. "What about that dolly in the shop? That yours?"

I turned to look at it. It was pretty beat up. The most recent paint job had been red, but chips all over the thing revealed that it had been blue, brown, and orange at various points in its history. I shook my head. "I've never seen it before in my life. They brought it with them."

Glenn opened the back door fully and looked into the alley. "Let's step outside for a moment."

I followed and he shut the door. The alley was empty, and the first light of dawn was coloring everything with a peachy pink glow. He evaluated me with a steely gaze. "You're in danger, Charlotte. I think it's very likely that they intended to go upstairs and give you the same treatment they gave Trevor and Mike."

I gasped. I hadn't even thought of that. I'd been so focused on Trevor.

Glenn continued, "I've had the pleasure of hearing a Great Pyrenees bark. I know you keep your dog very well behaved and obedient. He's well trained. Anyone who didn't know the breed and came into your shop might think your dog is just a big, fluffy marshmallow, nothing but show. But you and I both know that's not true. Those dogs were bred to take down wolves, and when they're triggered, they're intimidating as any pit bull. I think when the perpetrator heard him bark, they panicked and fled the scene before they could accomplish their goals."

A lump formed in my throat and I couldn't swallow it down. The weather was mild today, more springlike, but I felt a cold that had nothing to do with ambient temperature. I'd been affected by Mike's death. It had definitely frightened me. But now I felt terror.

"What should I do?" I asked, my voice coming out more timid than I'd intended.

"It's time to get serious. If you have the funds, a full-blown security system including cameras on the back alley and in the store would not be overkill. Continue with the guards as well. Trevor's presence here kept them from getting to you. And I'll put officers on this block around the clock."

"Why do they want *me*?" I wondered aloud.

Glenn exhaled forcefully. "I don't know. But I'd be willing to bet they think you know something that could be a clue to their identity. If you have any idea what that might be, don't hesitate to pass that along to me."

"I don't know anything!"

He ran his thumb and forefinger over his mustache. "It's either that or they have some kind of vendetta against you. Today their goal may not even have been to kill Trevor. They did start to cut him loose, after all. They may actually be after ruining your business."

I frowned. "I didn't see a drop in traffic after Mike... "

"No, but now you've had two violent crimes committed on your property. That might affect your insurance. Insurance companies get a little cranky about risk assessment. I wouldn't be surprised if your premiums double or even triple. That would easily put some stores out of business."

I hadn't thought of that. I must have looked pale, because he said, "The security system and cameras should mitigate some of that."

I nodded slowly. "I'll have them installed as soon as possible."

Becca's voice sounded from behind me. "Stegman's Secure Systems is on their way right now. I ordered the deluxe package. She'll have top-of-the-line cameras, door and window monitors, all of it."

I turned. Becca stood at the back door, dressed in her severe business attire with makeup and hair precisely in place.

Glenn nodded politely toward her. "Good thinking, Ms. Cordery."

"I'm sorry to interrupt, Charlotte. But your employees are starting to arrive. Should I send them home?"

"Yes, if you would, please," I said quietly.

This was a nightmare. The police seemed to be no closer to finding the murderer, and now they were coming after me and people who worked for me. I wondered how long it would take them to regroup and try again. If a security guard wasn't enough protection, would a security system even help? Wouldn't they keep looking for opportunities to hurt me and mine?

And what about the community I'd built around my business? All this chaos and death might keep people away, and while that worried me financially, it also worried me for the groups of students, businesspeople, and knitters who met in my store. Would they find somewhere else to go?

I stared at Glenn, doubts flooding my mind. I knew he was doing his best, but what if that wasn't enough? The killer had worn gloves. They were obviously intelligent, the way they'd planned this whole thing out. The stack of boxes, pretending to be UPS. That wasn't a spur-of-the-moment emotional endeavor. It was carefully premeditated.

And why? Why me?

What could I possibly have done to make them fixated on me?

Suddenly, following Vincent and searching for any clue I could find didn't seem so silly. It was time for all hands on deck, trained professional or not. The murderer wasn't satisfied with just killing Mike. They were going to keep coming and coming and coming.

And there was a target on my back. I had to do something.

Chapter Twelve

IT HAD BEEN three days since the attack on Trevor and so far nothing untoward had occurred. Trevor had been thoroughly checked out and declared to be fine. He was taking some time off, which I thought was a good idea, and we were rotating through some new guys.

I finally had a moment to breathe. No one had called in sick. Restocking and cleaning had been done. The morning's deliveries had been put away. Orders had been filled. I had a brief window of time before business picked up again.

I wanted a nap.

Instead, I had a quad-shot latte in my hand. I eased into my chair and leaned back, taking a big gulp as I savored the relief in my knees from having a seat for the first time that day.

Harvey got up from his bed and put his head on my thigh. "Need some attention, buddy?" I asked as I ruffled his fur.

I fired up my desktop computer and accessed the security-camera footage. I both hated this and appreciated the fact that it was there. Abingdon was a small city in rural Iowa. I shouldn't have felt unsafe.

I was adjusting to the new security system, but slowly. A

creature of deeply ingrained habits and routines, I kept forgetting to disarm it before using the back door. I'd triggered it several times, hurling myself into panic mode as I frantically tried to punch in the code correctly before it summoned the police. And then there were the times I'd thought I'd turned it on, when I actually hadn't. Gina double-checked it each night and patiently walked me through the procedure several times. It needed a red and a green button, for Pete's sake. It was too complicated.

Things were slowly getting back to a new sort of normal, outwardly at least, but inwardly my constant sense of unease wouldn't let go.

And I didn't think it would for a long, long time.

It had been bad enough when the target of what had seemed like a random act of violence was someone from within my community. But when it was me? Or people working for me? It wasn't random anymore.

And Glenn was asking me for anything I could think of that might connect the dots. That meant the police didn't have much to go on. Even with new evidence, I was worried they weren't any closer to ending this.

I didn't know how to process that. And while those around me probably thought I was doing just fine, in my head it was messy.

My chest felt tight with anxiety, pretty much all the time. I rolled my head on my shoulders and did some deep breathing, trying to loosen up. I gulped the high-octane coffee and began to review the footage. There were four camera angles dividing the screen into quadrants. The security guard watched these live every night, but in case he missed something while taking a bathroom break or doing rounds around the store, I felt I had to do my due diligence and review them myself. I kept it in fast-forward mode and watched an entire day at a time, only slowing the footage down if something caught my eye that seemed out of the ordinary. So far there'd been little that concerned me—just some rats hanging around the dumpster out back, for whom I'd already called an exterminator.

My eyes glazed over as I watched. I worried that I'd miss some important information just from sheer boredom. That was, of course, what the quad-shot latte was supposed to help prevent.

Then I saw something.

I backed the scroller bar up and clicked on that single camera view so it went full screen. I needed to see it bigger. This feed was from the camera mounted on the corner of my building looking down the alley in the opposite direction from Trance and Ganache. A few buildings down the block, basically at the edge of the viewable area, someone was fumbling with the lock on a door.

The lighting was dim because it was the middle of the night. The figure was shadowy, barely noticeable against the background. I wasn't surprised at all that the security guard had missed it. Despite that, with the image enlarged, the movements the person made were recognizable. They kept at it for a long time, bent over for a while, then getting down on their knees. And they kept looking around as if nervous someone might see them.

I got a sinking feeling.

It looked like they were breaking into the back door of that store. I squinted, trying to figure out which store it was. I decided it had to be the antique shop, Abingdon in Review. Though it was mostly filled with old junk, I knew there were a few things in that store that commanded a high price tag. I'd wandered through it myself more than once.

As I watched, the person stood, dusted themselves off, and picked up a tote bag I hadn't noticed before. I wasn't sure what they were doing at first, until I recognized the telltale signs of looking at a cell phone. I could clearly see the person—a woman—as she wandered closer to my camera, holding her phone up, trying to get a signal.

She came a few steps closer and I remembered what Mr. Stegman had said about being able to get a limited zoom. I paused the video in a place where she was facing the camera, found the right command shortcut written on a slip of paper taped to my computer case, and punched it in.

Oh.

The result was grainy, but I recognized her. It was Andrea Blankenship, Mike Blankenship's sister.

To say I was freaking out would be putting it mildly.

I remembered how I'd wondered aloud if Andrea could have murdered her brother, just a few days before. A frisson went down my spine.

Trance had already opened back up for business. It had been a short mourning period, but I couldn't really talk. I'd kept my store open throughout most of this ordeal. Of course, I hadn't lost a family member. But I also knew many of the businesses on this street operated on a knife-edge. She may not have had a choice unless she wanted to abandon the business entirely, especially since she was down one tattoo artist, her brother, who presumably had been the star everyone wanted to see.

And of course I was thinking about the fact that she'd already done time, and the stereotype of the criminal who picked up tricks and tips while they were in jail to use when they got out. I really hated that those things ran through my mind. People were not stereotypes. They were individuals. I reminded myself of the nice things Gina had said about Andrea.

Nevertheless, I was itching to call Abingdon in Review and ask if they had anything missing today. Or call the police and show them this footage.

One thing held me back—what had happened with

Vincent Pradel. Just like with him, there might be an innocent explanation for this behavior that I simply wasn't clued into.

I held onto that thought and clicked play on the footage. She must have gotten a signal, because she spoke on the phone briefly and then went back to the door. She fiddled with the lock some more, then went inside.

I looked at the time stamp. 12:52 a.m. I watched for a while. Six minutes later, two other people—they looked like women as well, also carrying large purses or tote bags—went in through the unlocked door.

Several women, working together. Could they have also worked together to murder Mike and to make the attempt on Trevor? Could this be some form of organized crime?

There was a long period of inactivity. Two hours almost exactly. At 3:01 a.m., all three women exited and walked away from my camera, the way they'd come, away from my store. I couldn't get a good image of the other two women.

What on earth was I looking at?

I paced back and forth the few steps available to me in my office. Maybe I should just go to the police with the footage. Let them figure it out. But what if I brought someone who was innocent under undue suspicion? Someone who was already reeling from her brother's death? That would be a lot of stress to put on Andrea. Stress she might not deserve.

There could be a simple explanation that I hadn't thought of. Just like with Vincent.

Darn it all. I was turning into an old busybody. And I was far too worried about other people's actions.

The only person I can control is me.

With that in mind, I left my office and signaled to Gina. It was late afternoon. Trance would be open. And I wasn't going in alone. I was going to be smart about this. And I'd take the pepper spray my sister had just given me.

Yes, I was getting increasingly paranoid.

"Yeah, boss?" Gina said with a grin as she approached. She was holding up remarkably well. When I'd asked her if she wanted to go stay with a friend somewhere else for a while, she'd reminded me that she grew up in a poor neighborhood in Chicago. She said she knew how to look after herself, and her jaw had been set. Her affinity for morbid T-shirts suddenly made sense. She'd lived through things like this before. It wasn't going to scare her off. And she wasn't going to leave me alone.

I glanced around the store. Two college kids were behind the counter, and one was talking to a yarn customer. The one making drinks was new, but picking the routine up quickly with occasional help from the rest of us. I thought these three could handle it if Gina and I stepped out for twenty minutes.

"You said you've hung out with Andrea Blankenship before," I said. "Do you know her favorite coffee drink?" Andrea never came into our store. I was guessing she didn't have money to burn on fancy drinks.

"I know she hates coffee," Gina quipped. Before I could respond, she continued, "But she does like chai lattes."

"Could you make one for her, the way she likes it? I'd like to go next door and talk to her for a few minutes, and I'd like you to go with me."

Gina looked confused, but she didn't ask any questions. I grabbed a spray bottle of sanitizing solution and a clean towel and wiped down already-spotless tables while I waited. My whole body was buzzing. It wasn't from the caffeine I'd just drunk. I was physically sick with anxiety. I didn't want to do this, but I knew I had to.

Gina caught my eye by holding up the drink when she was done, and I met her at the front door.

"Is this a community-building mission? Trying to put the past behind us and start fresh?" she asked.

"Maybe," I replied. I didn't want to cast a shadow over Andrea unless I had something more concrete. "I hope so."

We walked out onto the street and the few paces to the next building over. I put my hand on Trance's door and hesitated. "Could you humor me and dial the police department but not press call? Just to have it ready in case we need it?"

Gina's eyebrows drew together. She looked a little annoyed with me, but she held up her phone. "I've got the number on speed dial."

Smart girl. "Okay, that's probably good enough." I glanced back at her one more time before pulling on the door handle.

She was looking down at her phone and her expression got downright angry. She stabbed a finger at the phone.

"What's wrong?" I asked, releasing my grip on the door.

Her nostrils flared. "Jacob will *not* stop. He keeps texting and calling. He says he wants me to move in with him temporarily—platonically, of course. He says he's worried about me, wants to protect me. *As a friend.* He's such a child. Who says that? And maybe I'm getting paranoid, but I could swear I saw him tailing me on my way to campus yesterday."

Now I was upset too. "Have you gone to campus police yet?"

She sighed. "No. It's fine. I'm just too busy to put up with his crap right now. There's some political stuff going on in my department... yada-yada. Everyone's in a tizzy and its narcissistic gossip city over there right now among the grad students. It'll blow over soon. It better." She ran her hands through her hair and avoided my gaze.

"After we're done here, take the rest of the day, with pay, and go take care of that."

She looked skeptical, like she didn't want to do that. "Charlie, what are we doing here? What's going on?"

I took a deep breath and decided to ignore the fact that

she'd just changed the subject. "Paranoia. Confusion. Maybe redemption. Let's talk about it after we talk to Andrea."

Her brows raised to her hairline.

I pulled open the door. "After you." Then I whispered, "Stay alert."

Inside, the shop looked very different from the last time I'd been there. The lighting was brighter. The whole place was cleaner. All of Mike's devil and dragon art had been taken down and replaced with soft watercolor-looking artwork depicting things like a unicorn wearing an astronaut helmet, a beautiful black woman holding a sci-fi gun, a rocket ship trailing rainbows, and an octopus and a mermaid sharing a hug. There were small collections in a Japanese kawaii style too. Little cartoon characters doing cute things smattered all around. All very vivid and bright, a stark contrast to Mike's black-and-red art which had made the place feel like a demonic realm.

It was downright cheerful. I liked it.

There was a young couple seated on a couch going through albums that I had to assume were more tattoo examples. Another young man was sprawled on his back on a reclined chair that looked like it belonged in a doctor's office. Andrea sat on a tall stool next to him, bending over him with the tattoo wand in her hand, pots of color on a stainless-steel rolling table at her side. She was working on his shoulder, and I could hear the buzz of the machine as she drilled ink into his skin. She worked a bit with the tool, then stood and wiped his skin gently with a pristine white towel. She hadn't noticed us yet.

The fact that there were three other people here, plus Gina, made me feel a lot better.

"Hey, Andy," Gina called, holding up the chai latte. "Charlie and I brought you something."

Andrea dabbed the young man's shoulder again and

backed up a step, still looking at his arm, then looked over at us. "Oh, hey girl. That's cool."

"You've made some changes in here, finally got some of your own stuff on the walls. It looks fantastic!" Gina said. She continued wistfully, glancing back at the art displayed on the wall, "I'm still saving up for that unicorn. I can't wait until I can afford it!"

"I have some new stuff in that book on the counter." Andrea gestured with the cup Gina had just handed her.

Gina went over to look and immediately started oohing and ahing.

Andrea looked at me with frank curiosity. I felt awkward.

Her client said, "Are we taking a break? 'Cause I'd love to take a break right now."

Andrea shrugged. "Sure, if you need to. Can I get you a pop?"

He sat up slowly. "I'd rather have something stronger."

I wasn't sure if he meant coffee or booze, but I was going to assume coffee. I crossed the room, fishing in my apron for the cards I had in there. I handed him one. "Why don't you go next door and get a coffee on me?"

That would buy me a few minutes.

"Just a sec," Andrea said. She took a large square of gauze and carefully taped it in place over the ink on his shoulder, then smoothed his short shirt sleeve over that.

"Wow. Thanks!" he said. And he was out the door in no time. He must have meant coffee.

I tried to see what he was getting on his shoulder, but I couldn't figure it out in the glimpse I got before Andrea covered it. Gina and the young couple were still looking at the art books.

Andrea took a deep swig of the drink we'd brought. "This is soooo good," she remarked. "So much better than instant."

"Andrea, do you think we could talk privately for a minute?" I said.

She shrugged again. "Sure. Whatever." She turned and walked into a back room.

The walls were lined with industrial shelving and stacked with boxes of supplies. There wasn't a door. It was open to the store, but it was as private as we were going to get, I guessed. I licked my lips, suddenly unsure how to begin. I should have thought this through more, but I had been afraid I'd lose my nerve.

She looked wary. "What's up?"

I went with honesty and kept my voice low and quiet so no one would overhear. "First, please let me give you my condolences. I'm sorry about… what happened."

She nodded and averted her eyes. "I know you tried like hell to save him. Thank you for that."

I swallowed hard. "I feel really weird coming over here, Andrea, but I saw something today and I wanted to talk to you about it. I know it's probably nothing. I don't want to jump to conclusions. Gosh, I hate feeling like an old busybody—"

"Just spit it out." Her brows were raised in disbelief and her tone was humorous, but kind.

I nodded. She was right. "Well, I'm sure you know what happened in my store a couple days ago. I had to have a security system installed. With cameras."

My mouth was so dry.

Gina wasn't far away. I was just talking to someone. Clearing something up.

Andrea had a look on her face that was the equivalent of the word *So?*

"The footage it recorded last night showed you in the alley. It looked like you were picking the lock on the back door of Abingdon in Review."

I got the words out. I really hated confrontation.

She rolled her eyes and shook her head, then sat down on a step stool with one foot up on the first step. She looked relaxed, not at all like someone who'd just been caught doing something criminal. I began to have doubts about my theory.

"I might as well have been picking it. That stupid lock never works. It gives me fits every week."

I was watching her very closely. Something in her manner made me unwind a fraction more. "Every week?"

She looked like she was on the verge of tears. She sniffed and stood. "I don't like people knowing about this, but I guess I better prove it to you so you don't call the cops on me." She turned and rummaged in an open box.

I'm not proud to say I braced myself in case she had a gun in there, my hand slipping into the pocket that held the pepper spray.

No, she didn't have a gun.

She pulled out a… shirt? No, a smock. On the breast was embroidered the logo for Abingdon Cleans.

It clicked into place. Of course. I was so dense. "You're a cleaning lady?"

She looked disgusted. "I gotta eat."

I nodded, chastened. "Sometimes we have to do things we don't like to make ends meet."

"Ain't that the truth. And while Mike ran the place I had to maintain the illusion of a badass lady who does ink. The ex-con part doesn't hurt when it comes to that, but it's not me. Not really. Not at all. Cleaning lady doesn't fit either. If people found out I cleaned houses and businesses, they'd laugh at me. Mike always did." She had a hangdog look that made me feel so uncomfortable. I felt like I'd done wrong.

"I'm sorry, Andrea. He shouldn't have. That wasn't fair."

"May he rest in peace," she said. "But he was a jerk. There was a good guy inside there but he had a devil on his shoulder.

He gave in to that devil too much. I tried to help him see that, but he was also stubborn as a mule."

I didn't know what to say. "It sure seems like that was the case."

"He was a fool," she spat. "But I still miss him like crazy." She swiped at her face. "I was trying to keep him out of trouble since the day we were born. The devil and angel twins, they called us, when we were little. You know I took the rap for him when we were eighteen? I went to jail for him."

My mouth flopped opened with surprise. "The drug charge?" I said.

"It was his. Well, his supplier's. Said he needed someone to 'hold it' for him for a few days because the cops were snooping around. Mike had been slapped on the wrist so many times, but when the cop was coming up to our car, he was blubbering like a baby. That time he was sure he wouldn't be able to get out of it. Turned out he knew more about it than I did. My record was clean. I'd never tried anything harder than Lipton tea. I guess I thought I'd be the one to get a slap on the wrist that time. So I told the cop it was mine. I was young and stupid. It didn't matter that I was a good girl. There are minimum sentences for possession of hard drugs. I got five years. Served two. Screwed up my whole life trying to protect him and look what it got me. He's dead and I'm circling the drain."

"But you're not," I insisted. "You're doing your best."

She looked proud for a moment. "I just got my GED, finally. Gina helped me with that, you know. I want to go to community college to learn how to run this business better, maybe go to art school, but I don't know if I'll ever make enough to get ahead. It's expensive."

I thought about suggesting something about grants and loans, but I wasn't sure if someone with a record would qualify.

I decided I'd look into that and see what options I could find. Gina might know of something too.

An awkward pause settled between us.

Suddenly she blurted out, scorn written all over her face, "I wish the cops would just arrest Ben Davies and get it over with. It's taking too long. I told them he was the one who did it, killed Mike. He probably went after your guard too, though who knows why."

"Ben?" I was shocked. "Wasn't he Mike's best friend?"

"For decades. But love and hate aren't that far apart. You should know that."

She wasn't wrong about that. "But he's such a sweet guy…"

"Sure he is. But sweet can spoil. Go sour. Mike and Ben were definitely on the outs. I don't know what happened between them because Mike never told me, but whatever it was, it was serious. Here's what I do know. Ben and Lauren decided to stop drinking a few months ago. No exceptions. All of a sudden. Mike was… Let's just say he was unhappy. He liked having things the way he wanted them, and he wanted his drinking buddy. And he seemed to think that the not-drinking business was Lauren's idea. He'd never liked Lauren, anyway. So things were already tense. Mike was treating Lauren even worse than usual, which got Ben's hackles up. I don't know what finally triggered it, but I walked into the middle of them having a knockdown, drag-out, no-holds-barred fight. Mike was missing a tooth, needed stitches, and was limping for two weeks after that."

I was stunned. "Ben told me they'd had a fight… I never would have imagined it was physical."

"I thought they were going to kill each other. You should have seen them. It took me forever to break them up, and I got a black eye out of it to boot when one of them grazed me with a stray punch. I was the lucky one who got to clean up all the blood in here. It was splattered everywhere like a fricking crime scene. They both should have gone to the ER. I know Mike didn't, but I don't know about Ben. I told the police about that too. Said if he went to a doctor, there should be some kind of record of that fight, but why would they listen to me? I'm nobody. Less than nobody. But I do know this—that if you can beat a man bloody, and you're mad enough, you can kill him. I may not be that smart, but I know people—how they work. I've seen things in all these years, between jail and running with Mike, that would curl your hair."

I didn't doubt that. "Did anyone else besides you see that fight?"

She shook her head. "Just me."

I was lost in thought when Andrea shoved a card into my hand. It said Abingdon Cleans on it and had an address and phone number. "No skin off my nose if you call them for verification purposes. The police already did. I had to give them an alibi for the night Mike… passed. I've been cleared. I have multiple witnesses for my whereabouts at the time of the crime. The lady who owns it understands. She knew about my record when she hired me and she's nice about it. At least someone is."

I tried to hand her back the card. "I don't need to call her. I believe you."

She wouldn't take it.

"You keep it. You might decide you need someone to clean, and it's a good service. Fair prices and they pay us fairly too."

I shoved the card into my jeans pocket. "Good to know. If I ever need anyone, I'll call them."

I heard the voice of her young male client back in the shop. I said, "I better let you get back to work. Thank you for talking to me about this and not getting mad about it."

She shrugged. "No problem." She started to walk past me.

I had a sudden idea. I reached out to her but didn't touch

her. She stopped. "Hey, I'd like to help you if I could. I've got some wall space in my shop. How would you feel about putting up a little art installation and setting out some cards or flyers about your work?"

She looked stunned.

"A lot of people would see it every day. You could add new artwork anytime you like."

"Why would you do that?" she asked.

"Because I like your art. I like to help people. I want other women to succeed. We aren't in competition. Our services are complementary. Or they could be."

She smiled shyly, and for the first time I got a glimpse of the girl inside her—the girl who hadn't been beaten down by bad luck and circumstance. "I like that. It'll take me a few days but I'll put something together. Thank you."

"Good. And don't hesitate to reach out to me if you need help. I'll be here for you, if I can. We women in business need to stick together."

"So you aren't going to buy this building?" she asked hopefully.

"No. I have no plans to expand my shop at this time."

She grabbed my hands. "Thank you. I think I can make it, but only if I can keep expenses low."

I pressed her hands warmly. "That's the mantra of small business, Andrea."

I ambled back into her store.

Andrea's client raised his coffee cup. "Hey, thanks! Great coffee!"

I pulled out a handful of the same cards I'd given him and handed them to Andrea. "Give one to your new clients. A little perk. Added value."

"Thank you. I will."

Gina and I walked outside. "So, what's the verdict? Is it redemption or more suspicion?"

"Definitely redemption," I replied.

And I was back to the drawing board.

Ben Davies was now firmly planted at the forefront of my mind. Andrea had just given me some new information to explore. I needed to know more about the fight between Ben and Mike. What would cause two best friends to brawl like enemies? And was it a motive for murder?

Chapter Thirteen

THE FIRST THING I did after returning from Trance was to give Glenn Swinarski a call. I asked if he could verify that both Andrea Blankenship and Vincent Pradel had alibis for the night of Mike Blankenship's murder. I told him they'd both verbally conveyed that information to me and I needed to know if it was true. Before I even gave him a chance to speak, I told him I no longer felt safe talking to just about anyone because most of the people I saw every day were suspects. He hemmed and hawed and then confirmed the alibis in a sort of roundabout way, without coming out and saying it plainly.

Guilt. Becca had been right. Moms know how to use it.

So that meant that both of them had been officially taken off the suspect list.

I, however, had not. I didn't have an alibi. I'd been alone in my apartment the night Mike had been killed. He didn't specifically say whether I was a suspect in Trevor's assault or not.

I also didn't ask.

Any evidence against me was circumstantial. I had faith in the justice system. Unless the police found something that had been planted to frame me that they weren't telling me about, I should be fine. That wasn't likely, I didn't think.

Glenn wouldn't tell me any more about the investigation than that, though he was awfully polite about it.

Well. Hm.

I thought a lot about the things Andrea had told me. Who would know Mike and his associates better than his fraternal twin, who worked with him every day? Her comments held weight with me, and I hoped the police were taking her seriously as well. I stopped myself just short of saying as much to Glenn. It wasn't my place to tell him how to do his job.

I began to wonder whether there was more to Ben Davies than met the eye. I thought of myself as an excellent judge of character, able to see through duplicity and guile. I was a mom after all—a darn good one, I'd always thought. I'd tried awfully hard at that job.

But maybe Ben was one of those people who was really good at deceit. Maybe he'd honed those skills all his life. That would explain why Mike had liked him so much. Perhaps their relationship wasn't the opposites-attract sort after all.

It was certainly possible that he'd fooled me with his sob story of lacking motivation and goals. He could have skillfully played into my own particular weaknesses, my desire to help people and see the best in them. He might be adept at telling people what they wanted to hear, at being the person they wanted to help. Some people skated through life doing that.

That didn't necessarily make me gullible or stupid. It just meant he was very good at it.

I certainly couldn't imagine the Ben Davies I knew participating in a brawl that drew blood and left someone battered and missing a tooth. That was the detail that bothered me the most.

I wanted to know more—bad enough that I was considering sniffing around, even after my rather substantial gaffes with both Vincent and Andrea.

Andrea thought Ben was the murderer. That didn't jive with what I knew about Ben. But neither did the fight Andrea described. And she wouldn't have any reason to invent that detail that I could imagine. So, I decided it was time for me to find out more about Ben. I already knew he didn't have an alibi. He'd told me that himself.

If I discovered anything of note, I'd pass it on to Glenn. If I didn't, then I'd just spent time in the pursuit of truth. There was nothing wrong with that.

It came down to this: I trusted the police to do their jobs. But whoever had killed Mike Blankenship wanted me dead as well, and I wasn't about to sit on my hands and wait for them to accomplish what they set out to do while the police worked on narrowing down their immense list of suspects. Andrea was right—it was taking forever for them to bring someone into custody, long enough that the killer had already committed a second crime.

Poking around might put me in danger, but I was already in plenty of danger.

Constantly messing with the stupid security system, security guards coming in every night, pepper spray in my pocket, Gina with the police on speed dial, my sister taking over my apartment and keeping me from sleeping properly—none of these things would let me forget that my life was in jeopardy. Not for a minute. There were reminders everywhere.

Frankly I was sick to death of living in fear. I had to *do* something.

I started in the early afternoon by driving to Balser Electric, the electronics factory where Ben worked. I didn't know where else to begin. I had only a vague idea of what I was doing, but it seemed worth a shot.

There was a red-and-white-striped arm across the entrance

to the factory parking lot and a guard at the gate cut in the ten-foot chain-link fencing. The guard came out to my car holding a clipboard. I pushed the button to make the car window go down.

"Gotta badge?" he asked.

"No, sir. I—"

"Applying for a job?"

I hesitated. "Yes," I said.

I had to get in somehow.

The guard took down my name and phone number and asked for my driver's license to copy the number. He pointed out exactly where I was allowed to park, handed back my license, and waved me on. "Office is on the second floor."

"Thank you."

The place was noisy. And really warm, despite the cool temperatures outside. I tromped up the grey-painted cement stairs to the second floor. I couldn't have walked out into the main factory even if I'd wanted to. There was a metal door and a badge scanner. Clearly no one went in there without a badge.

The office was disorganized and sort of grungy. There wasn't a receptionist at a desk. Maybe they were out for a late lunch. It sure seemed like I'd come at a bad time. I hung back, watching and waiting for someone to notice me.

The offices were lined on two sides with windows, so I had a view of most of the work floor. I watched people working while I waited. Some operated big machines. Others sat at stations doing piece work, taking parts out of a box on one side, modifying them somehow, and placing them in another box to their other side. Another group moved things around the floor. Big metal items on carts and stacks of boxes on dollies.

Dollies.

I took a step closer to the window, peering down carefully.

Those dollies looked familiar. Mostly red, but with severely chipped paint revealing multiple layers of other colors underneath—blue, brown, and orange.

Great googly-moogly.

Surely there were millions of dollies in that condition all over the U.S.—but in that specific color combination? I'd have to tell Glenn about that. It seemed very likely to me that the dolly used to hurt Trevor in my store had come from the Balser factory.

This was a clue. An important one.

The charming Ben Davies was looking more and more guilty.

"You here for the interviews?" someone asked in a tired and bored voice.

I whirled around, caught off guard as I'd been concentrating so hard on staring at the dollies as they zoomed by. "No, actually—"

"No?" The guy looked surprised and irritated. He was older, wearing a dress shirt and slacks, which I thought probably marked him as management. His salt-and-pepper hair was cropped short, he held a grubby stack of file folders filled with paper, and his badge hung from a retractable clip on his belt. I couldn't make out his name unless I moved to his other side. He was pretty nondescript otherwise, aside from a worn-down, hassled air.

"I'm sorry to bother you. I just have some questions."

He sighed. "Reporter?"

I smiled tentatively. I'd lied to get in on impulse. I was beginning to worry that might get me in trouble. "Not that either. I have questions about one of your employees—Ben Davies."

"If Ben has applied for a job with your company, there are specific forms for that. We don't give personal recommendations anymore. Haven't for years. It's too much of a liability."

I bit my lip. "No, it's not like that, either."

"Look, lady, unless you're with the police, you've got no business being here. If you're after gossip, then you're in the wrong place. Go across the street to Libby's after a shift ends and you'll hear all the gossip you could ever want."

"Oh, is that where your employees go after work?" I asked, still keeping my voice light despite his obvious annoyance. I wasn't getting much out of this guy, but that tidbit could be helpful.

He blinked real slow. "I think that's what I just said."

"Okay. Thank you for taking the time to talk to me."

He walked away, grumbling under his breath. I hurried out to my car before he called security on me.

I thought the guard at the gate would just let me out. I was wrong about that. He came around to my side of the car. I rolled the window down again.

"Ms. Shaw, you look like a real nice lady, but you're gonna get yourself in trouble if you run around pulling stunts like this. I just got cussed out by the head honchos upstairs for letting you in here."

"Well, I did lie to you," I squeaked.

"You sure did. Now, I'm a nice guy, so I'll do you the courtesy of letting you know that this incident will be reported to Abingdon PD." He tapped my hood. "You stay out of trouble, young lady."

"I'll try," I said, and drove through as soon as he lifted the gate. I made a right and immediately got in the left-turn lane to pull into Libby's 24-Hour Diner.

For research purposes. With a side of pie.

Most of what I needed on a daily basis was within walking distance of my apartment in downtown, so I didn't get across town very often and hadn't been to Libby's in a long time. But everyone knew that her diner made amazing pies. I wasn't the least bit put out by having to find a reason to legitimately spend some time there.

At least this time I didn't have to lie.

A nice slice of caramel apple pie might be just the thing to get my heart rate to slow and my blood pressure to come down a few notches. I was already worrying about what Glenn was going to think or say regarding my visit to Balser. Of course, maybe he'd never know. It might be the kind of thing that some officer recorded in a database and no one else ever saw. I didn't think it was the kind of thing a person got arrested for. At least I hoped not.

Libby's was empty except for a big guy in a ball cap sitting on a stool at the counter. It was a seat-yourself kind of place, so I chose to sit on the other side of the room in a booth. There were two paper placemats on the table, covered with advertising for local businesses, as well as two napkin-wrapped sets of silverware, and two overturned coffee cups on saucers.

A waitress approached holding a full pot of coffee. She was about my age, blonde—probably bottle blonde, but expertly done —and had her hair up in an artfully messy updo like the kids like to wear it. She wore a retro waitress outfit that was neat as a pin, and the name tag on her shoulder said her name was Alice. Her makeup was skillfully applied, no small feat on an aging face. I could never make mine look that good, which was why I'd given up on it years before. She looked cheerful, a nice contrast to the guy I'd just seen at Balser. "What can I get you? Do you need a menu?"

I eyed the coffee in Alice's pot, wondering how long ago it'd been brewed. The place was dead so it might be old, but it was a full pot so maybe she'd just made it fresh. Yes, I am a coffee snob, but I decided to risk it because sweets always taste better with that bitter brew's counterpoint. "No menu for me, thanks. I'd love to have a coffee and a piece of caramel apple pie, if you please."

"Alrighty." She turned my coffee cup over and poured. "You want it warmed?"

"No, thank you."

"A la mode?"

"Nope. I'm a purist when it comes to pie. Do you get a lot of business from Balser?" I jumped straight into my reason for being there before she bustled away.

"Don't you know it. I'm bracing myself already," she joked.

"What time does the current shift let out?"

Alice glanced at her gold-toned wristwatch. "First shift will start coming in about five minutes from now, but I'll get you your pie before then." She winked and turned away.

She was back with the pie less than a minute later. In the meantime I'd been thinking. It was almost 2:00 p.m. now. As she set it down, I asked, "So does the second shift let out at 10:00 p.m.?"

She nodded solemnly. "Yes, ma'am, unless they're working mandatory overtime."

"Have they been doing that lately?"

She looked up at the ceiling, thinking. "Not the last few days, no. But they work them hard a lot of the time."

"Will you be here at ten?"

She pulled an impressed face, batting her eyes. "My word, you are just full of questions! But the answer is yes. I work three twelve-hour shifts a week, so I get the pleasure of two Balser rushes every time I come in." She leaned in conspiratorially. "Second shift tips better."

I smiled. "Do you ever see a young man named Ben Davies come in here?" I wasn't sure what I was fishing for, but I was going to keep casting a line until something bit.

"Oh, yeah. He's a cutie pie. Doesn't come in nearly so often since he went off and got himself a girlfriend. Used to be a regular, but not anymore." She looked a little pouty.

I was feeling the same. I'd hoped… Well, I didn't know what I'd hoped for.

Through the window I saw three cars pulling up and a bunch more lining up in the turn lane. Alice was about to get too busy to talk to me.

"Do you know who his friends are? Do they ever come in?"

She leaned over, one hand on the back of the booth, the other on the table, her voice going softer and her eyes wide. "Well, you know that Mike Blankenship just got murdered. Last week, I think it was. They used to come in late at night sometimes after Mike closed down his shop, or even later, after they'd been drinking."

"What about Ben's other friends? Is there anyone he works with that comes in regularly?"

Her eyes drifted to one side and I got the feeling that she'd just realized that this was more than just friendly conversation. "A few. Why do you ask?"

I opened my wallet and set out what would have been an overly generous tip for a family of four. "If I come back at ten, and they're here, will you point them out to me?"

"Lady, are you a cop?" she whispered.

The bell above the door kept ringing, and people were coming in left and right. It was time to let her go.

"I'm… investigating something. Will I see you at ten?"

Alice snatched up both of the twenties I'd laid out and sent me a side-eyed look. "You want change?"

"No, ma'am."

She flashed her teeth at me conspiratorially. "See ya at ten!"

The coffee was pretty meh, but the pie was delicious.

Chapter Fourteen

I GOT out of my vehicle at Libby's at 9:50 p.m. I'd been sitting inside my parked car in the dark thinking of strategies and talking points for over ten minutes. Just a continuation of my thought processes as I'd dragged myself through the last eight hours.

I'd spent the rest of the afternoon in the shop, taught a beginning knitting class early in the evening, walked Harvey after close, then told Becca I had an errand to run without revealing my purpose or destination, or giving her a chance to ask about it.

My stomach was in knots. I still wasn't sure if I was doing the right thing, but the prospect of doing nothing seemed even worse. So there I was.

Lying to the Balser gate guard that afternoon hadn't sat well with me, but I thought I'd have to continue that trend to stay safe. I decided to tell Ben's friends, if they showed up tonight, mostly the truth with a few embellishments to make my interference easier to digest. I needed them to be open and honest, not defending their friend. If I framed the conversation like I was trying to clear Ben, they'd be more receptive.

The diner was busier than I'd expected it to be for 10:00 p.m. There were booths of loud-talking college students, blowing off steam. A few couples. Several trucker types and possibly a farmer or two, seated at the counter. Even a family with little kids struggling to get through their meal without a meltdown.

The booth I'd taken earlier in the day was open, so I sat down there, laying my coat next to me. Alice was bustling back and forth, taking orders and bringing out drinks. She waved when she saw me. "Be right there!"

After a few minutes, she sidled up to my table. "Good to see you again. What can I get you, Mrs. Shaw?"

I hesitated. I hadn't given her my name earlier in the day. Abingdon was small, but not that small. I'd be lying if I didn't admit I felt a jolt of a good old-fashioned dose of freak out.

"Oh," she said, laughing, and thumbed toward the cook at the grill behind the counter. "Amos recognized you. He says his wife drags him into your shop pretty regularly." She sat down across from me and splayed her forearms and hands flat on the table. "Before it gets busy, I wanted to ask if you have any shifts open in your shop? They'll only give me three days per week here. I don't knit, but I do crochet. And I could use the money."

Based on what I'd seen so far of her performance, she'd fit in well with my employees. She was bright, she had hustle, and she was extremely pleasant with her customers. I liked having a mix of ages and backgrounds among the people I hired. They tended to learn a lot from each other, and not just about the work we did. Whatever she didn't know about coffee or yarn, she could learn.

And if I wasn't going to expand the store, I could afford to hire another person to take some of the pressure off me, just like Becca wanted me to do. "As a matter of fact, I do. Why don't you come downtown and fill out an application when you get a chance?"

Her eyes twinkled. "Will do." Then she got more serious. "I have a feeling I know what you're up to tonight, what with Mike Blankenship's death and the police dragging their feet and all. I can see why you feel motivated. Just be careful, okay?"

I nodded solemnly. I felt pretty safe in a diner full of people, but she was right. I needed to be wary.

She rose from the booth like a girl half her age. I wished I still had that kind of energy. "Can I get you anything while you wait?"

I didn't have any appetite, and I wasn't risking that coffee again. "How about a diet?"

"On its way," she called over her shoulder as she took off.

She brought the pop a moment later and flitted off to check on her other customers. It wasn't long before I could see headlights across the street and a stream of cars starting to make their way out of the gate, many of them pulling into the diner.

The folks coming in looked tired and were relatively quiet. I watched Alice carefully as I sipped my pop. She worked the tables efficiently, with a smile for every single person. I noted that she never wrote down orders. She memorized them and ran back to the cook to call them out after every table. The other two waitresses carried around order pads. That kind of memory would be useful in my shop.

The line of cars streaming out of Balser's lot petered out, and the diner was nearly full to capacity. After Alice had taken all the orders from her assigned tables, she returned to my booth. "The guys in the corner work with Ben Davies," she said, gesturing over her shoulder toward a round corner booth. "And they all ran around in the same gang with Mike. Do you want me to introduce you?"

A wave of anxiety flooded my system, but I tried to sound normal. "No, ma'am. No need for you to get involved. I'll take it from here." I stood shakily with my purse and pop, then turned to grab my coat. I hovered there a moment, not sure whether I wanted to crowd the booth with that too, if they'd even let me sit down.

"I'll take that off your hands," Alice said. She grabbed my coat and scurried to the back of the diner, where there was a coat rod, and hung it up for me. Then she went off to pick up some of her customers' food from the grill.

I put one foot in front of the other and headed for the young men at the corner booth. They were a good-looking bunch, all late twenty-somethings. A little rough around the edges, making choices according to their age group, status, and affectation like every generation did. In this case that meant sporting tattoos, piercings, colorful hair dye and so on. They had that familiar look of people you saw around town, but I didn't know any of them by name.

It occurred to me as I surveyed them that Ben had a slightly different style. Unless you saw him in a sleeveless tee, you wouldn't necessarily know he had tattoos. And he didn't have any other visible body alterations. That allowed him to move easily through different social circles and marked him, at least in my mind, as being extremely smart. But what kind of smart was he? Savvy smart or sneaky smart? I was hoping to find that out.

All three of them were staring at their phones. I stood there with my purse over my shoulder, holding my pop. "Hi there, fellas," I said, smiling nervously.

Only one of them lifted his gaze from his phone. "Hey," he said, uncertainly, setting his phone down. His hair was a faded aqua color, and he had small gauge earrings in both ears. His clothes were worn but clean. The front of his tee dipped low enough that I could see he had a tattoo on his chest, though I couldn't make out the design. He nudged his buddy next to him, who dragged his eyes up from his phone to stare at me. The second guy had that cultivated straggly look. Dark, curly hair and beard, both a little long and unkempt. The few small rips in his clothes were probably for effect, not because he couldn't afford untorn clothes.

"Ah… I know you don't know me, but I'm a friend of Ben Davies. I'm told you guys are too. I wondered if you could help me with something."

The first one to glance up looked skeptical. "How do you know Ben?"

"You know the coffee shop next to Trance? I own it. Ben comes in a lot, so we've been friends for a few years." It was a bit of an exaggeration, but they probably wouldn't clue into that. I hoped.

"What do you want?" the second guy asked with a cynical look on his face. He seemed annoyed that I'd interrupted his phone time.

"Goodness!" Alice came up behind me. "The nice lady just wants to talk to you. Scooch over and give her some room!"

Surprisingly, they did. I perched on the very end of the curving seat, tucking my purse beside me and setting my pop on the table. "I won't take up much of your time. Ben's in trouble. I'd like to help him clear his name, but in order to do that, I need to know more about him."

They continued to stare at me blankly.

"My name's Charlie, by the way."

The first one to notice me gestured at himself. "I'm Travis." He pointed at the other two guys. "Mark and Curt."

"Nice to meet you—"

"Why don't you just talk to Ben?" Mark asked as he brushed his shaggy hair back from his face with fingers adorned with ink as well as heavy silver rings, some of which bore the shapes of skulls and other menacing things. I noticed he also had some tattoos on his arms which resembled Mike's style.

I hesitated for a second. It was a good question. "I have, and I plan to again. But sometimes when we talk about ourselves we paint a prettier picture. If I'm going to figure out the truth, I need to see the *bigger* picture. Look, this whole thing with Mike Blankenship and his murder is happening around me—and affecting me and the people I care about. I need to find some answers."

Curt hadn't put down his phone. His dark hair had been bleached at some point—there was a stripe of dull orange fading into white at the tips—and he had large-gauge, stretched-ear-lobe piercings you could see through, as well as full colorful sleeves of ink, which I guessed had also been done by Mike. He didn't look up, but said, "That sounds like the cops' job to me."

"That's true," I retorted. "But in case you hadn't noticed, Mike messed with a lot of people. I'm guessing they're busy chasing down a whole bunch of leads. It's going to take a while for them to narrow down their list of suspects. In the meantime, that puts a lot of stress on Ben—being a suspect when he's already grieving about Mike."

Travis looked thoughtful. "That's for sure. He's been staying at my place a lot, and the dude's been pretty gnarly lately."

That was a surprise, given that I was pretty sure he and Lauren had a place together.

Mark grunted agreement. Curt kept his eyes on his phone, occasionally typing with his thumbs at an incredibly rapid pace, his longish nails tapping the screen. He clearly didn't like me being there and was determined to ignore me for the most part. I wondered who he was texting.

"You work with him at Balser?" I asked, and took what I hoped was a nonchalant sip of my pop. It wasn't that I was afraid of them because they'd done all these body modifications. I'd met a lot of kids who did that—like my boys' friends. At the end of the day, it was just another personal choice of a different generation. What I was more afraid of was not getting any good information from them because they saw me as… well… the elderly enemy. I considered complimenting their appearances, but figured they'd see that as a form of apple polishing. I was sure it would backfire, especially with Curt, who seemed very invested in the badass persona he was cultivating.

Travis leaned back and rubbed his hair. "Yep. Second shift in the warehouse."

"Were any of you with him the night Mike was murdered?"

One side of Travis's mouth turned down and he shook his head. "High key—the police already asked us all this stuff. No one we know saw him that night."

High key? Hm. I didn't know that one. I decided to try a different tactic. "Whenever I see Ben, he's a perfect gentleman. Is that what he's like all the time? Or is that just the way he treats ladies of a certain age?" I smiled a little, hoping a self-deprecating comment would help my cause.

Mark snorted. "Sure. He's always like that. When he's not drinking, that is."

I raised my brows, inviting them to elaborate.

Travis said, "That's pretty much it. Once he gets some booze in him, the pretty boy you'd take home to mama is gone."

"So when he drinks he gets…" I trailed off, hoping they'd play mad libs with me.

"Salty," Mark said.

Travis frowned. "He gets snarky. Cocky. Says things he wouldn't say otherwise. And he doesn't know when to stop."

So that was why Mike liked him so much, especially as a drinking buddy. Together they could rile things up. I'd just learned something I hadn't known. That felt good. I needed to press on for more details. I was being pretty direct, but they were still answering, so I kept it up. "Do you think that's why he and Lauren stopped drinking?"

Mark shrugged. "Probably."

"Did that improve their relationship?"

Curt made an inarticulate sound and rolled his eyes.

Travis glanced at his friends then back at me. "No one likes Lauren but Ben."

That didn't surprise me.

Mark said, "It didn't seem like it. Things got worse than before."

"That's odd. Has Ben mentioned why he's sticking it out with her?"

All three of them looked at each other like that was obvious, so I decided to let that topic lie. I wasn't interested in prurient details. I felt my face get warm. "Did you know that a couple of weeks before Mike was killed, Ben and Mike had a big fight?"

Andrea had told me she'd been the only witness, but I didn't think it hurt to ask.

Alice arrived with their food. Burgers and fries for all three. They dug in immediately, clearly ravenous after their shift.

Travis swallowed a big bite and wiped his mouth on his paper napkin. "No one saw the fight, but Ben told us about it. He was pretty messed up."

"I heard Mike lost a tooth," I commented.

"Sounds about right. Ben sprained a finger or something. He had some cuts and bruises," Mark said, then wrapped his mouth around his sandwich.

"Were they fighting about Lauren, do you think? Or about the drinking?" I asked. I wasn't surprised Andrea didn't know —being the opposite gender from her brother might have made him reticent about such things. But other young men who hung out together would talk. I'd seen that with my own boys when they didn't know I was listening. It wasn't for the faint of heart. I was counting on that now.

A trio of shrugs and covert glances was my answer.

"You really don't know? It could be important," I prodded in my best mom voice. It was a risky tactical move. It could shut them down entirely, since I was a stranger. *Ahem. An elder stranger.* Or it could get them talking due to societal conditioning. I hoped for the latter, though I wasn't sure with this group, considering their antisocial lean.

"Lauren," Mark said around a mouthful of food.

"Mark," Curt said in a reprimanding tone.

"What? It's the truth!" Mark said, spewing bun crumbs. He gave Curt a gentle shove.

"It's not a nice topic," Travis said, not meeting my eyes.

"I'm still listening."

Travis wiped his mouth again and set his napkin in his lap. He'd had good training, which might be paying off for me now, I hoped. He looked down at his plate, with his fingers and thumbs positioned on each side like a frame. He pushed the plate forward a couple inches then turned to me. "Mike had a bad habit of sleeping with his friends' girlfriends. There aren't many of us that hasn't affected over the years."

I raised my brows and felt my cheeks get even warmer as I contemplated my next question. "Are you saying Mike slept with Lauren?"

"No one knows that for sure," Curt said sternly.

"But everyone thinks so," Mark piped up.

"Mike hated Lauren, especially after Ben and Lauren stopped drinking," Travis said carefully.

There was something he wasn't saying. I eyed Travis. "And?"

"And Mike bragged to me that he did it," he admitted quietly.

"What?" Curt said.

"No way!" Mark all but shouted.

Mike sleeping with Lauren might have been Ben's motive.

Travis continued quietly, "I guess he figured he'd prove a couple of points to Ben. So one night while Ben was at work, he got her drunk and slept with her. Then he let it go for a while. Weeks, I think. Let her think she was off the hook. Told her he'd never breathe a word. But the minute she slipped up —made some snide remark—he told me. I think he knew I'd tell Ben."

"Did you?" I asked.

He sighed. "Yes. The night they had the fight. I thought he should know. I was trying to be a good friend."

"Dude," Mark breathed. He shoved himself back on the bench like he was stunned. "I never thought Mike would do that to Ben. They were so close."

Curt finally put down his phone. His expression softened. "I wonder if Lauren knows that Ben knows."

I thought back to the day I'd spoken to Ben in my shop and something he'd said to Lauren. "I think Lauren knows that he knows."

Curt's eyes widened and I saw the boy within. All the badassery had fallen away.

"Unfortunately, none of this helps clear Ben. It only makes it look worse," Travis said, with a forlorn look on his face.

Yes, it did. But his friends clearly thought he was innocent, based on their reactions.

Mark leaned forward, grabbed a handful of fries, and dunked them in a pile of ketchup. "What are you going to do now?"

"I don't know," I said honestly. "Probably talk to Ben." I couldn't think of anything else I *could* do, aside from telling Glenn everything I'd learned. But maybe he knew all this already.

Curt had picked up his phone again. "You're in luck," he said sarcastically. "He just pulled up."

I huffed in amused disbelief, even while trepidation rose inside. "Is that who you were texting?"

Curt shrugged one shoulder. "He's my bro. I don't know you, lady."

"Fair enough." I rose and grabbed my purse. I pulled out some business cards and set them next to my empty diet pop, along with a twenty for Alice to cover the pop and another generous tip. "I'll go talk to him now. Please let me know if you think of anything else that would help Ben."

Travis eased his plate back toward himself. None of them said goodbye or anything more. They just looked relieved that I was leaving.

I got my coat. I didn't think Ben would want to talk about these things in a diner full of people. I certainly hadn't been comfortable doing it. So I'd talk to him outside—in full view *of* the diner. I waved to Alice as I shrugged on my coat.

Upon exiting the diner, I double-checked my jeans pocket for the pepper spray. I had no idea how Ben was going to react to the questions I had to ask him.

Chapter Fifteen

I STOOD outside Libby's and let my eyes adjust to a much lower level of light, making a show of putting on my gloves and scarf. That gave Ben a chance to see that I was there, and I wanted to bundle up if I was going to be standing outside for any length of time. It continued to be a cold spring.

I heard someone sniff and turned my head toward the sound. Ben stood leaning up against a car parked next to my own. I liked where he was standing, actually. If I joined him there, we'd be in full view of half the diner. And the parking lot was busy with customers coming and going. If there was a struggle—if I screamed—someone would hear. That made me feel a lot safer.

The door to the diner opened behind me, so I headed toward Ben to get out of the way. I couldn't see him well enough in the sparse lighting to tell what kind of expression was on his face. Would that pleasant facade be gone? Would he be angry? I waited until I was closer to say anything.

I kept my voice low so it wouldn't broadcast across the entire parking lot. "Hi, Ben. I understand Curt texted you to let you know I was talking to him, Mark, and Travis."

Ben let out a shuddering sigh. I was close enough now to see that he looked bewildered. "What is even going on?" he said. "Why are you interrogating my friends?"

"Interrogation is a strong word," I said, and immediately regretted it. It put him on the defensive. His nostrils flared. "Look, Ben, this is serious. Someone killed Mike and they nearly killed a security guard. The police think they meant to kill me too. Meanwhile, I'm a suspect. I'm just trying to figure things out."

"Do you really think I did it?" His voice sounded mournful, like I was the last person on Earth he'd want to think he was guilty. Was that an act? Or the truth?

I kept my reply noncommittal. "In learning the truth about Mike, including your interactions with him, I might be getting closer to figuring out who the murderer is. I think… I think people will tell me things they wouldn't tell the police."

He sniffed again, but otherwise didn't reply.

My eyes had fully adjusted. I could see that he was skeptical, but I didn't see any trace of menace. I remained uneasy nonetheless. "There's something you don't know, and I'm not going to tell you the details because I promised Glenn Swinarski I wouldn't. But whoever the murderer is has made an attempt to frame me for it. I don't think the police are buying into it, but between that and Trevor Fontenay—it's personal."

"Jesus," he breathed. "I didn't know."

He seemed so sincere. I reminded myself about the yarn, the dolly, the fight over Lauren. "No one does."

"I didn't do it, Charlie, I swear!" He sounded desperate.

"Can you prove that? So the police can take you off the suspect list and can focus on finding the right person?"

"I don't have an alibi. I can't prove anything," he choked out.

"What did you do that night?" I asked.

He seemed to be reluctant, but I kept staring with my most formidable mom-stare.

"I was drinking, okay? I got completely drunk all by myself and passed out." His voice was a bitter whisper.

"I need more details than that if I'm going to discover the truth, Ben," I said.

"You aren't going to judge me for my stupid mistakes?" He lashed out like a truculent teenager. It reminded me of how young he was. So darn young that he thought I'd care if he drank or not.

"No. I just want the truth."

"Fine. Not that it matters. I didn't even tell the police because it's not going to help me. I'm supposed to be off the booze. I've had two OWIs, and now I've got a freaking breathalyzer on my ignition. I can't afford any more trouble with the police. I was stupid. Upset about something with Lauren. I went to the Dunk, but they wouldn't serve me because Mike and I had been in too many fights in there. So I... You know that little grocery store nearby?"

"The Piggly-Wiggly?" I prompted. I knew it well. A friend of mine owned it.

"Yeah. I walked in there and bought a fifth of Jack and went back to my car. I didn't have anywhere to go, so I just sat there and drank it until I passed out. I woke up in my car the next morning."

So he *was* on the outs with Lauren, if he didn't have anywhere to go before he started drinking.

"How much did you drink?" I was attempting to discern if it would be enough to bring out his rougher side. I purposely didn't mention that even if he hadn't driven the car, simply being in a motor vehicle while drunk could have gotten him another OWI in Iowa if the police had noticed him. The laws are very strict about that. I'd lectured my boys about it more than once.

He glanced at me sideways. "Not all of it. Though not for lack of trying. My car smells like a bar."

Now I had something I might be able to work with. I'd talk to him about getting help later. A lecture wasn't going to fall on receptive ears right now, so I kept probing for truths. "Where was your car parked?"

"In front of the Piggly-Wiggly," he said.

I had an idea for how I could check his story. I pulled out my phone to see the time. There were missed calls but I ignored them. It wasn't quite eleven yet. I might make it, if I left right then. I was more than ready to end this conversation and get in my car and drive someplace far away from Ben, where I'd feel a lot safer. "That helped a lot. I'll let you know what I find, but it might not be until tomorrow morning." I handed him one of my business cards. "Text me at that number so I have yours. Can't explain now. I've gotta go."

I hopped in my car and drove off, leaving him standing there in Libby's parking lot looking like a deer caught in headlights.

I hit mostly green lights and arrived at the Piggly-Wiggly with five minutes to spare. While driving I'd heard my phone buzz a few times, but it wasn't until I was walking into the store that I glanced down long enough to see a text from Ben, like I'd asked for. As I walked up to the automatic doors I noted a sign in the window, just like one that now graced my own shop: *This property surveilled by Stegman's Secure Systems.*

Marci had the good stuff.

I went straight to the checkouts. There were two clerks there, one still helping the last stragglers of the night and the other closing down her register. I popped into her field of view. "Is Marci upstairs?" I asked.

"Yep," she replied.

I headed for the stairs behind the empty lotto-and-cigarette counter like I owned the place.

My oldest son Blaine had dated a young woman named Penny all through high school and into college. They'd eventually broken up for reasons he'd withheld from me, but while they were together, our families had gotten close. That was how I knew that Penny's mom would probably be upstairs.

Marci owned the Piggly-Wiggly. Like me, she kept odd hours. She might be in and out of the store all day, but would definitely be nearby at both open and close most days. She'd actually been a huge inspiration to me when I decided to open my own shop. I'd seen how she'd arranged her life and felt that if I could replicate her approach, it was something I could do too.

The upstairs offices were still lined with wood paneling. Since customers never saw this part of the store, Marci had no reason to update them. A worn-out copy machine sat in the corner of the hallway, with a few boxes of paper towels stacked on top. I slipped off my coat, threw it over my arm, and knocked on her office doorframe, a big smile on my face.

It was good to see her again. Marci was probably a few years older than me, but time had been kind to her. She had an athletic body type and kept her dark brown hair in the shaggy feathered hairstyle that had come into fashion in the eighties. She was a pretty average-looking Midwestern woman of inscrutable age.

Marci turned away from her computer, and her face transformed into something joyful. "My goodness—Charlie! It's been a while!" She leapt up to hug me.

"Too long," I said.

"How are the boys?" she asked, holding me at arm's length after the warm hug.

"Good. Too darn far away for me to see them often enough, but good. And how's Penny?"

She rolled her eyes and smiled. "Same. I don't know why they all think they have to move away."

"Maybe they'll come back when they're ready to settle down more permanently. At least that's what I keep hoping."

She pointed at me. "I like that. So what brings you out here so late at night?" She gestured at an office chair nearby and I sat down, shoving my gloves in the pockets of my coat and my scarf in one of the sleeves.

"I'm sure you know about the murder behind my place," I started.

"Yes—are you okay?" Her kind face was suddenly worried. "I really should have called… "

I waved her off. "For the most part. A friend of mine has come under suspicion. He doesn't have an alibi—unless you can help me find one."

She sat up straighter, ready to get down to business. I had always liked her. "How can I help?"

"This is a young man with some issues. He says that the night of the murder he came into your store and bought some alcohol and then went out to his car and drank until he passed out. I was hoping one of your cameras picked him up parked out front."

If she took issue with Ben's behavior, she didn't say anything about it. She immediately called up the Stegman software on her desktop, like I did every day. "Let's see," she said. "The murder was in the early morning hours of March 7th, is that correct?"

"Yes."

"Soooooo… let's start looking for him on the sixth before we closed." She punched a few keys and then clicked intermittently with the mouse, navigating to the right place in the video storage. Eight camera feeds came up on her large monitor. Mine only had four, but of course her store was much bigger. I could see one for the front parking lot, one for the rear delivery area, and six at various spots inside the store. She clicked on the feed that captured the front parking lot, and it filled the screen. "Any idea what time he came in?" Marci asked.

"No. Sorry."

She put the feed in fast-forward and slowed it down whenever someone came in, so we could see their faces. At the time-stamp of 9:58 p.m., I saw him. "That's him," I said, rising in my seat a little. I was excited. I guess I was relieved that Ben had been telling the truth. Maybe my instincts about him hadn't been wrong after all.

"Okay… " Marci clicked back to the main view with eight cameras again. We watched him buy whisky and what looked like a package of powdered donuts. "That was probably his dinner," she said wryly.

"Probably," I confirmed.

As we watched him leave, she maneuvered back to the camera out front. She was good at this. It was clear that she'd done it before. She might have to deal with things like shoplifting and credit-card theft on a regular basis. I grimaced.

Then we watched him through the windshield of his car. Drinking. And drinking. And drinking some more. Then he ate the donuts. More drinking. He stared off into space for a while. Then he went slack against the headrest. And he stayed that way, relatively unmoving, until morning light, when it seemed as though he tried to start the car with the breathalyzer, failed, then got out of the car and stumbled away out of sight.

There it was. Ben Davies's alibi.

He couldn't be the murderer. I slumped in relief. Ben didn't want to kill me.

Marci stood and went to a filing cabinet. She rummaged through it and came out with a thumb drive still in its package. She broke it open, stuck it into her computer, then told the computer to save the video to the thumb drive.

I was watching the save bar grow across the screen when

she laughed and said, "Charlotte Shaw, please tell me you aren't dating this young man."

I gaped like a fish out of water. "What? Me? Oh, no. No, no, no, no, no, no, *no*."

She pulled a hand across her forehead. "Whew. I was worried there for a minute."

I started laughing and had a hard time stopping. "Oh, my goodness," I said through giggles that made my words all but unintelligible. "No. I'm not dating. *Anyone*. No plans to. At all." I was crying I was laughing so hard.

When I finally slowed down, she said, "You know that wouldn't be such a terrible thing, Charlotte. You deserve some comfort."

Comfort? I thought back to my failed marriage. It felt like a lifetime ago now. Maybe in the beginning he'd been a comfort to me. But by the end, our time together had been about little more than *hostilities between us, our mutual state of near*-constant grumpiness, and our frequent loud disagreements. I'd lived for years with the perennial feeling that he wished I was something or someone else. It had been constant *dis*comfort. "That's not… " I floundered.

"You might have better luck this time, if you're careful," she said. Her face was full of kindness, and I was feeling the irony of the role-reversal. I was usually the one doling out advice to the people in my life. "It's hard, when we're young, to choose a partner that will suit us forever. None of us are very smart at that age." She gestured at the computer screen where the save bar indicated the download was almost finished.

I got the point.

"I'll think about it," was all I could muster. The very idea ran counter to my lived experience. The divorce still hurt, even after ten years. Starting over with someone new sounded like torture. But I would think about it.

Marci turned, clicked a few things with her mouse, pulled

the thumb drive out of its port and placed it in my hand, then covered my hand with her own. "You're being very brave, helping this young man and the police, but be careful, Charlotte. The world still needs you."

I nodded solemnly, then leaned over and picked up the empty thumb-drive package from her desk. "Can I pay for this downstairs?"

She waved me off. "I buy them by the case. At wholesale. It's nothing. Consider it my contribution to your cause."

I stood and slipped the thumb drive into my purse. "Thank you. I'll let you get back to work. We should get together more."

She tilted her head. "You know, people say that a lot and never do it. Let's make a date right now."

I smiled. "I like how you think."

We settled on a date. I wrote it down on a slip of paper from my purse and put it in my pocket to add to my calendar later. We hugged warmly, and I set off down the stairs and back into the store, where I had to wait for one of the cashiers to unlock the door to let me out.

Back in my car, I pulled out my phone to send Ben a message. "I have what you need. Don't tell anyone about this. Not even Lauren or your friends. It could be dangerous. Come see me tomorrow at the shop."

I was back to square one. Again.

There was a text from Becca, wondering why I was out so late. I'd normally be in bed by now. She was probably annoyed that I'd left her home alone with Harvey. It made me realize just how late it was and how tired I was getting. I predicted a massive quantity of coffee in my future the next day.

On my way home, I texted back, and closed the app.

The little red numbers next to the phone icon reminded me of the buzzing I'd ignored earlier. I tapped that app. It was actually one missed call and a voicemail. I didn't recognize the number, so I put the voicemail on speaker.

Oh. My stomach flipped over.

It was Glenn Swinarski. About the factory.

It was late. I'd call him back tomorrow.

Chapter Sixteen

HARVEY and I walked around downtown early the next morning. We stayed close to home and only in the brightest-lit areas. Walking him had always been one of my greatest joys, but now it felt terrifying. I jumped at every little sound and kept looking over my shoulder to see if we were being followed.

Adrenaline kept the fatigue at bay just as well as the best Ethiopian Yirgacheffe.

Despite all I'd learned, I wasn't any closer to figuring out who the murderer was. I knew it wasn't Vincent, Andrea, or Ben, and those had probably been the police's chief suspects originally. Eliminating them made me feel better, but I still didn't have any evidence to take to the police that pointed to the actual murderer.

Harvey stopped at a public trash receptacle on the street and got to sniffing. It was directly under a streetlamp, so I took the opportunity to double-check our surroundings. Aside from the occasional car passing on the street, we were alone.

His tail swished back and forth as he evaluated the leavings of other dogs around the base of the receptacle, which had been raised off the ground on a short pole. I noticed something in his tail glinting in the light.

I stepped closer, pulled off my gloves, and captured his tail between my fingers. "Did you pick up some glitter, buddy?" I asked as I parted the long, trailing strands and tried to track down the source of the shine. I hadn't brushed him properly for a few days. I'd been too busy. Now I felt guilty for neglecting my duty. If I wasn't careful, he'd develop some mats and dreadlocks. His fur was as soft as cotton candy and easily tangled.

My fingers clamped down on something bigger and harder than I expected. It took a few moments to extricate it from his fur. "What on Earth?" I muttered aloud as it finally came free and I held it up to the light. Harvey ignored me and kept on sniffing the base of the trash bin before he finally added his contribution to the doggie mélange of liquid deposits.

It looked like an intact fingernail. Or actually... I turned it in my palm. Like the press-on nails that had been so popular during my teenage years in the eighties. Except this was really fancy. It had little studs and rhinestones and lavender glittery polish on it.

I had a sudden flash of memory. Lauren's nails looked something like this. Maybe even *just* like this. One of the last times she'd been in the store I'd noticed it. And then another surge of memory came to me... Marilyn remarking that Lauren had done her nails once and they'd "popped off" in less than twenty-four hours. Is this what Marilyn had meant? I didn't know anything about this nail stuff.

I lifted my coat and stuck the nail carefully in the tiny front pocket of my jeans. I patted Harvey and headed back home. "Where did you pick this up, Harvey?" I asked him.

There was no way to know for sure. And it couldn't be counted as evidence. I knew that. But I suspected that it might have flicked off one of the fingers of the murderer in my office when they were getting Trevor in my chair or tying him up. They'd been wearing gloves, but the tips of gloves were known to break easily, especially if punctured by a stiletto-shaped fake nail. The police hadn't found it when they searched my office, but Harvey's tail was like a dust mop. It picked up everything—and he'd been in the room with Trevor moments after the perpetrator left. The police hadn't checked his fur for evidence.

I'd asked Glenn if they were going to bring in a forensic team, like on TV, but apparently Abingdon wasn't big enough to have one of those, so police detectives had done that work instead.

It could have been a random nail Harvey picked up on the street or in the store.

But somehow… I didn't think so.

Lauren would have had access to all the same things I'd thought pointed to Ben, through him.

And the same motive.

Was this Lauren's nail?

Back in the store, I put the nail into a little baggie and fell into my routine like a zombie, but my mind never strayed far from it and how I could use it to discover more evidence.

Gina helped me open the store as usual, but the spring in her step just wasn't there, and I noticed her stifling yawns. "Trouble sleeping last night?" I asked her. I wondered if Becca's snoring could be heard in the apartment below.

"No sleep," she said flatly. "There's been a problem with one of my students. I'm all embroiled in stupid department politics, and Jacob is still texting me on the regular. I didn't mean to, but I was so mad I ended up staying up all night playing. It was medically necessary."

I blinked. I didn't understand the video-game-as-therapy thing, but it seemed to work for her. Maybe I should try it. Shooting imaginary arrows or fire bolts at fantasy creatures when I was frustrated might feel good. Then again, maybe not.

If she stayed up all night playing, that hinted at an addictive quality to gaming, which I already suspected had Gina hooked. "Do you feel better?"

"Yes, but now I'm tired." She looked resolute. "And I'm not going in to the university today. I don't have anything pressing and the thing with my student seems to be resolved, even if I don't agree with the method of resolution, so I'm going back upstairs to sleep as soon as Angie comes in. I'll make up the time later."

I nodded and patted her arm, resisting the urge to ask her if she had gone to the police about Jacob. I'd made my opinion clear and I was not going to harp on her. "I think that's a good idea."

When I saw Marilyn walking down the street toward the shop, I made her a coffee that was ready as soon as she walked in the door. I held it up and gestured for her to sit in her favorite chair. She was our first and only customer so far, just like most days.

"You better stop treating me like a queen or I'm gonna start expecting it," she teased.

"Get used to it," I said. "You're a queen among women in my book."

I pulled the nail from my pocket and sat down across from her while she settled in. She took some reading glasses from her purse and got her knitting arranged on her lap. A nearly-finished navy blue wool charity hat on four double-pointed needles, from the looks of it. It would keep somebody much warmer sometime in the near future.

"Marilyn, you know more about nails than I do. Can you tell me what this is?" I held out my open palm, showing her the nail in its small plastic bag.

She picked up the bag gingerly and turned it in her hand to look close. "It looks like you went against my advice and got your nails done by Lauren Waters," she said.

I shook my head. "No, I just found it. It... this isn't a human nail, is it? It looks like plastic."

She looked at me and frowned. "You've never had your nails done?"

I smiled. "Nope."

"Well, in the industry I believe they would call this a nail enhancement. They're usually an acrylic polymer that they make by mixing a powder and liquid. That would be called an acrylic nail. Of course, some nail technicians these days use what is basically an ultra-violet-light-cured resin. They call that a gel nail."

"They put it over top of your fingernails?"

"Yes. To keep the nails strong so they don't break. That way they can be formed up nice and long if you want."

I nodded. "So they make this artificial nail over your real nail, and then they can decorate it with all this extra stuff?"

"Indeed they do. They can do regular polish or gel polish, and some nail techs embed those crystals and so forth if you want to pay a little extra for it."

"Is that common?" I asked. "This kind of crystal stuff?"

Marilyn looked thoughtful. "Not around here. You'll see it more if you go to Cedar Rapids or Des Moines. But most women in Abingdon have simpler tastes. I had my nails done like that once and I'll never do it again."

"Why is that?"

"Two reasons. One: Even if it had been done right, I didn't like the texture of it. It felt weird, and it was hard to get my hands into my pockets and so on. They got caught on *everything*. But the most important reason was that the nails didn't stay on my fingers. It was a waste of money." She chuckled.

"Who did them like that?" I asked, but I thought I already knew the answer.

"I told you—Lauren Waters. She's known for doing all kinds of fancy nail creations. That's all well and good, but you have to get the fundamentals down first or I'm not interested." Marilyn clucked her tongue to show her displeasure as she handed the nail back to me.

"You seem to know a lot about this. Do you have any idea if there could be DNA on this thing?" I remembered that Marilyn was a retired physics professor. She took an interest in all kinds of things. She might know more about DNA than I did.

Marilyn slid off her reading glasses and stared at me. "My word. This is more serious than I thought."

I grimaced. Marilyn was one smart lady. "It is, but I think it would be best if we kept this conversation just between you and me."

"No worries there, Charlotte. I won't tell a soul. To answer your question—there might be. Around the cuticle area a few skin cells might get picked up and adhered to the enhancement. But if the nail tech is good, they don't touch the cuticle at all. *And* a good nail tech will also put down some bonder and a base coat to help the artificial nail stick. Since this one didn't stick… that step may have been skipped. So if it's the person we're talking about, or one of her regular clients, it just might have some DNA on it. But I'm no expert." She leaned in. "Are you going to take it to the police?"

"No, I can't. I just found it in Harvey's tail fur. I have no idea where he picked it up. It just… it got me thinking."

Her lips drew up in a disapproving fashion. "I'll just bet it did."

"Do you happen to know when Phalanges opens?" I asked her, rising.

"Nine a.m. You going to sniff around and see what you can find?"

I looked down at my pathetic nails. I'd been biting them from the stress. They were an absolute mess. "Maybe. Maybe I'll just go and get my first manicure ever."

Marilyn grabbed my arm. "You be careful, Charlotte. I like you!"

How many people had said that to me lately? Of course, there'd been two violent crimes on my property in the last week. It was certainly warranted.

"I will. Don't worry about me."

I got back to work. Angie came in like a force of nature, launching immediately into restocking, cleaning, and serving customers, a reverse-tornado of order and efficiency. Gina plodded upstairs to go to bed without lingering.

I hadn't heard from Ben yet, but he was probably a late riser since he worked second shift. I wasn't going to return Glenn's call until I heard from Ben. That way I'd have something positive to say after he chewed me out for my stunt at the factory the day before. I wasn't sorry I'd done it. It had turned out to be a productive endeavor.

More than anything else, it proved to me that I was a good judge of character. And that momming other people could get results, when needed, though I wouldn't resort to it every day.

I looked up from wiping down the cream, sugar, and stir-stick counter to see that Alice had come in and was speaking to Angie about getting a job application. As I finished up, Alice was already seated and filling it out. I went over to the table where she was sitting.

"Well, that was fast," I remarked with a smile.

One side of her mouth pulled down. "Oh, you know. Money's tight these days. I've got time on my hands that could be better used working than doing crossword puzzles and crocheting granny squares. It's not always easy finding a good job where the boss is a nice person."

Apparently I'd made an impression. That felt good. "Well, I'll leave you to it."

She lifted one finger in the air and beckoned me closer. "There was something I should have mentioned last night when you were asking about Ben Davies," she said in a low voice.

I glanced at the nearby tables. People seemed to be either working on laptops or deep in conversation. Hopefully they weren't listening in. I folded the bar towel I was holding and sat down next to her. "What was that?" I was intrigued, but already sure Ben didn't have anything to do with the murders.

"It might pertain to what you're looking into, I think. It's not about Ben, per se, but his girlfriend. And that Mike Blankenship." She whispered the last bit.

"Oh? Lauren?"

I was all ears.

"I think that's her name. Like I said, Ben doesn't come in to Libby's much anymore, but I was there one night when that girl came in and met Mike. She's not… nice at all. Treated me like dirt. But that's the industry, you know. Sometimes we have to put up with that."

I nodded. I'd come across my fair share of unpleasant customers, though in general we were pretty lucky with our regulars. It was interesting that Lauren treated other women in the service industry with the same disdain that she treated me with. I wondered why that would be.

Alice rolled her eyes as she continued. "Just general nasti-ness. They sat in a booth in the corner. There was a lot of angry whispering. They were definitely arguing. And when I came by to refill their drinks, I could have sworn I heard the word *paternity*."

I felt my eyes go wide as saucers. "Goodness."

"That's not typical diner talk," Alice said, and looked back down at her application, pen poised to resume filling it out. "But that's all I heard. Do you think that helps you at all?"

I squeezed the towel in my hand. "It might. Thank you. I look forward to reading your application. I'll give you a call in a day or two."

It might help quite a bit, actually. There could be more motive in that tidbit than I'd known about before.

Alice smiled brightly and went back to writing.

I looked around the store. It was almost nine. Phalanges would be opening soon. Business was fairly slow and we had plenty of experienced people working, so I let Angie and the others know I'd be gone for an hour or two. I took off my apron and slipped out the door to see if I could get a walk-in appointment at Phalanges.

Chapter Seventeen

THE FIRST THING I noticed when I walked into Phalanges was how much I liked the decor. The color scheme was mostly black and white with bright pink and silver accents. The back wall was covered with three-dimensional wavy panels in fuchsia that undulated all the way up to the extremely high tin ceiling. At that end, there was a raised platform supporting several black chairs that looked almost like thrones. At the base of each was a small built-in tub which I assumed was for pedicures, rolling black stools placed in front of every one.

Crystal chandeliers provided warm lighting, while both side walls were lined with black desks and black chairs, each station with its own rectangular light fixture on a moveable arm. Framed prints featuring nail art of various kinds, all in pink tones, hung above the worktables, as did a large neon sign with the name of the salon in pink. A flamboyant touch, but it fit in with the eclectic decor.

In the front of the store, where I stood, there was a reception desk and a bright pink sofa. The walls featured narrow shelves bordered with ornate picture frame molding, painted black, each shelf displaying row after row of polish in every color imaginable. It felt elegant and cheerful. I wondered who'd done the decorating—and if I could hire them.

I seemed to be their first customer of the day. In fact, it was still just one minute to nine.

"Good morning!" a young woman said as she emerged from a back room. She had sleek, shiny dark hair, hanging to her waist. She smiled, flicking her hair over her shoulder, and looked at a book on the receptionist's counter. "Do you have an appointment?"

"No, I was hoping to make one. Do you take walk-ins?" I asked.

"Certainly. Manicure? Pedicure?"

"A manicure today."

She took down my name and phone number. "We can get you in right now, if you have time. Do you have a preference of who you'd like to work with?"

I took out my baggie. "Do you have anyone here who can do something like this?"

She extended her slender hand, and I noticed her nails were extremely long and impeccably coated in a bright-blue, iridescent polish. The length of her nails changed the way she held her hand and grasped the bag. I couldn't handle nails that long. How would I do anything? How would I knit?

"As a matter of fact, we do. That looks like Lauren's work. She's known for this kind of sparkle. No one else in town does anything quite like it."

Well, that confirmed what Marilyn had said.

The young woman drew her finger down the page of the appointment book. "You're in luck. Lauren is booked back-to-back all morning, but she does have an opening right now. Have you seen her before?"

"No," I admitted. I felt a little sheepish. "I've never had my nails done before."

"You're in for a treat then! Let me just go let her know

you're here. Please have a seat. Can I get you something to drink? Coffee? Tea? Pop?"

After the cold walk, something warm sounded good. But I bet they served pod coffee, and I couldn't bear the thought of that. "Some tea would be lovely."

The young woman brought out some hot water and an assortment of teas. I chose Earl Grey. Then I waited. Meanwhile other women arrived and began to receive manicures and pedicures.

I remembered something else Marilyn had said to me and downloaded Instagram on my phone. Lauren's profile was easy to find. I spent the next few minutes scrolling through the images she'd posted there.

It was all glamorous selfies and nail art. She was definitely a beautiful woman, and some of the designs were very pretty, though most verged on too garish for my taste. But half a million people followed her account, and each image had garnered thousands of comments. That was an impressive social-media presence. I began to understand why Phalanges kept her on even if there were problems. Where she worked was mentioned in the bio portion of her profile. It probably brought people into the store regularly.

My anxiety was growing. I felt out of place in this ultra-feminine environment, and I had no idea what I was going to say to Lauren to try to catch her. My amateur investigations had taken me down a bunch of dead ends. I didn't think I was very good at this.

I only had this stupid nail and my gut to go on. That wasn't enough to give to Glenn. Not if I wanted him to take me seriously.

I knew she had access to that pink yarn. And to a Balser dolly through Ben. She had an ax to grind with Mike. All the pieces fit. Now I just needed something more substantial.

As my nerves grew until my fingers tingled with pins and

needles, so did my resolve. I had to get to the bottom of this. Preferably before someone else got hurt. The police were taking too long. Whoever the killer was, they seemed to be willing to attempt to murder just about anyone they didn't like, or anyone who got in the way.

I heard heels heavily clacking across the room and looked up. I had just stopped scrolling through Instagram on a very damning image and had been studying it painstakingly.

Lauren had finally come out. She was dressed in a slim-fitting ivory turtleneck sweater and charcoal pencil skirt with low black boots. I furtively glanced at her abdomen. If she was pregnant, she wasn't showing yet, but with a first baby that didn't usually happen until about the fifth month.

She had a bored expression on her face, and she did seem a little paler than usual. She busied herself at one of the nail stations. She got out a clean black towel to cover the table and pulled out assorted tools, unwrapped them from their sanitary packaging, and adjusted the lamp a little lower. Then she put on latex gloves.

Trevor had said his assailant had worn gloves like that.

Then she went to the front desk and looked at the book. "Charlie?" she called halfheartedly.

I got to my feet and she looked at me for the first time. I watched her expression closely. She stared at me for a long moment. I saw a muscle in her jaw bulge from clenching. Then she forced a brittle smile onto her face. "If you'll just follow me," she said in a professional voice with the tiniest of edges.

I followed her, sat down on the black club chair at the station she'd been preparing, and set down my mug of cooling tea.

She seated herself, arranging things busily. I noticed her nails were a solid matte nude without any bling.

She'd changed them since the murder. And to something very different.

Smart girl.

Internally, I quaked. I might be seated across from a person who wanted me dead, who'd been intelligent enough to orchestrate all manner of things while flying under the radar. As far as I knew, the police didn't even consider her a suspect.

Was she smarter than me? Was I dooming myself by coming here?

I reminded myself I could be wrong—I'd been wrong three times already.

"And did you choose a color?" she asked, as if this was a thing she recited all day long.

I produced the baggie once again and held it out to her. "I'd like something like this."

I saw her eyes flare just the tiniest bit at the sight of it, and that telltale muscle flexing in her jaw. "That's very pretty," she said. "Where is it from?" Her eyes bored into me like hot coals.

I'd expected this, but it didn't make it any easier to endure. I tried not to squirm in my seat as my stomach flipped over. I wasn't going to survive if I didn't buck up. I had to pull from somewhere deep. "A friend left it for me," I said.

Her mouth twisted momentarily in scorn and then smoothed. "I see. What a nice friend."

She held out her hands. I set the bag with the example nail on my side of the table and extended my hands to her on top of the towel, willing them not to shake.

"Well, I don't have much to work with. You bite your nails." She tried to sound matter-of-fact, I think, but it came out sounding like an accusation.

Not the nicest tone for someone with such a social job. I wondered how she treated her normal customers. Was she always this haughty? Or was it just me she didn't like?

And why? Why did she dislike me so much?

I didn't respond to her quip. Instead, I said in my best

maternal tone, "How are you feeling these days, Lauren? I haven't seen you in the Tink Tank lately. Are you doing okay?"

She picked up a file and hovered it over my nails as she glanced at me. "Fine. Just fine. So, would you like an acrylic or gel extension?"

Now I was glad I'd spoken to Marilyn, or I wouldn't have had any idea what she was talking about. I tried to inject nonchalance into my voice, but I sounded meek to my own ears. "Either one. Whatever you're most comfortable using. Just not too long, please."

She sighed. "Squoval, almond, ballerina... ?"

Now that was a question I had no idea how to answer. "Whatever you think is best—just not pointy and not too long."

Then she was sawing at my cracked and frayed nail tips, pushing back my cuticles with a spatula-looking tool, and scuffing up my nails with the file. It didn't hurt. It just felt rougher than seemed strictly necessary. She wiped off my nails with a small pad soaked in something cold and opened a clear bottle with its own brush to drag something over my nails. It evaporated instantly and made my nails look chalky. She produced another clear bottle and brush. This one left my stubby nails looking glossy.

Then she opened a drawer, peeled a paper sticker off a roll, and applied it to my left pointer finger so that it fit under what was left of my natural nail, against the quick and folded underneath. It was a clever-looking contraption. I supposed this was what Marilyn had meant when she said they could form up a longer nail. Lauren repeated the process with the remaining four fingers on that hand.

I was just sitting there like a stooge. I had to move this forward.

"It's so awful, what happened to Mike," I said. "I know he and Ben were close. You must really miss him."

A beat passed. Then she said, "I do think Ben misses him."

That was an interesting evasion. Especially since I was confident she and Ben weren't living together anymore.

She looked like she might have been about to say more, but the young woman who'd checked me in came by and picked up the bag I'd left on the edge of the table. She studied it. "This is so pretty!" she exclaimed. "Didn't you have nails just like this last week, Lauren?"

Lauren shook her head. "No."

That was a lie. I was certain of it.

"Are you sure? I could have sworn you did. Even this very same shade. This is a ColourDiva gel polish, isn't it?"

Lauren suddenly covered her mouth with her hand and swallowed audibly. She gave another little negative shake of her head and eased her chair back from the table. She was looking a little green around the gills. "Excuse me a minute," she said, and dashed off to the back room, wobbling a little on her heels as she hurried.

I felt a moment of reluctant sympathy for Lauren. I had a feeling I knew what she was suffering from.

The receptionist seemed oblivious. She'd taken my baggie to the front of the store and was searching through the polishes along the wall, comparing them to the nail in the bag. After a few moments she came back triumphant. "See? This has to be the same shade. What a pretty lavender. So sparkly!" She set the bottle of polish down on the table top, along with my nail baggie, and smiled at me.

"It looks like an exact match to me. Thank you," I said. I moved the polish to Lauren's side of the table with a flourish.

"Perfect! Glad to help!"

When Lauren came back, the contour and blush on her cheeks were starker than they had been before. She brushed her hair back from her face and sat down. She seemed to be gathering herself back together. She clasped my left hand again. Her fingers were cold and clammy, like she'd just rinsed them with cold water.

She looked vulnerable. I felt like now was a good time to ask a question I wanted an honest answer to. Though it did seem a bit mean, I decided to do it anyway. This was my once chance—the one thing she'd let get through that was incriminating.

I pulled my phone out of my purse on my lap with my right hand and unlocked it. "I know you said you didn't have nails like this last week, but I saw this on Instagram. Isn't this you?" I asked innocently.

It was a close-up picture of her with a sultry expression on her upturned face. Her index finger artfully pulled on her lip. The lighting was fantastic and highlighted every detail. It seemed obvious to me that the ring finger was an exact match to my baggie nail. I set the phone on the towel so it was easy for her to see.

She stared at the picture blankly for a few moments. Then she got back to work. With shaky fingers, she squirted some liquid into a tiny glass container, sloshing it over the edge a little, and opened a plastic jar of powder. One or both of them had a chemical odor. It was the first time I'd noticed any strong smells in the room. They must have a good ventilation system in the salon.

Lauren wrinkled her nose. Then she turned her head into her shoulder and grimaced like she might cough or sneeze. She murmured to herself, "No, I think we'll do gel today."

She put those two away and pulled out another small pot full of odorless, viscous fluid. She produced a narrow, squared-off paint brush and began applying the gel to my nails in quick sure strokes. After completing each hand, she instructed me to cure it. I hesitated the first time until she pressed a button on a machine sitting on the desk facing me and a light came on inside. I realized I was supposed to put my fingers in there to be cured by the light, like Marilyn had mentioned. I left them there until the machine beeped and the light went off, then returned my hand to her.

"You look a little peaked. Are you sure you're feeling well?" I asked.

Her nostrils flared. "Fine. I'm fine." It was practically a growl.

She was concentrating hard, but as she paused between each nail, the paint brush trembled.

I felt like I had my answer. But I still didn't have any evidence the police could use. I tried another tack, keeping my voice light. "Abingdon is such a small city. I wonder, do you know Trevor Fontenay—the security guard who works for me?"

"No."

I decided to go in another direction, keeping my voice light in case we were overheard. "Ben works at Balser Electric, doesn't he? Do you ever visit him at work? Maybe bring him lunch or something?"

She stared daggers at me, but only for a second, before glancing around the room and returning to my nails.

"They've got strong security at Balser, but I bet the guards could be sweet-talked if someone forgot their lunch," I commented.

She didn't reply. I opted to try another tack.

"Do you like dogs, Lauren? You know my Harvey is such a cream puff, but when he's worked up, he can let out such a ferocious bark. It would just scare the pants off anyone who didn't know him."

She ignored me. I reluctantly admired her determination, even while I knew I was flying far too close to the sun.

And I still didn't have anything concrete that I could give to Glenn.

I was going to get myself killed.

I thought and thought about what I might say to her that would trip her up, but nothing worked. She was doggedly going to get through this without saying another word to me, without expressing a single emotion, if she could.

She had nerves of steel. I couldn't provoke her. And yet, I couldn't seem to stop myself. I had to learn something the police could use. "Don't you just love the smell of old books? Like at the library. They have sales a few times a year. I swear I'm tempted to just buy up a bunch of old books, just to have that scent around. Do you like old, heavy books?"

Nothing.

After she put the goopy stuff on every nail and I cured them all in the light, she put a dust mask over her face, aggressively tore off all the paper stickers, and we were back to vigorous filing. It seemed like she was shaping them just so. They were definitely longer than I wanted and seemed to be shaping up into squared-off ovals. Squovals? Was that the word she'd used earlier? But I didn't comment on that. I knew I was running out of time.

After a while, I gave up. I couldn't think of anything else that I could say in public. I knew for certain she'd lied about the nails she'd worn the week before. But I wasn't going to get a confession out of her. I wasn't the most savvy amateur sleuth in the world.

But I had rattled her. And unless her reaction to me was just pure old-fashioned hatred combined with morning sickness —admittedly, I suspected she was suffering from the latter malady—she was the killer.

And she knew that I knew.

In a room filled with lively women, all deep in their own conversations, I wasn't in immediate danger. She was too smart to do something then and there. But I'd just sealed my fate if I didn't come up with something damning, and fast.

She cleaned up the filing mess and moved on to polish. She

used the bottle the receptionist had brought to the table, bending over close to my fingers so I couldn't see her face. There was more light curing. Another coat. The light again. A clear coat. The light. Then she applied some more goo to my nails and painstakingly stuck rhinestones and silver studs to the goo. The light again. Then she squeezed a tube of oil, putting a drop of it on every cuticle. She rubbed that briefly on each nail.

And we were done.

She excused herself the moment she finished. I waited for a few minutes to see if she would come back. At the next table over, someone was getting a hand massage after their nails were done. But there would be nothing quite so pleasant for me today.

The nails were pretty and they seemed to be solid. I was glad I didn't have to wait for them to dry. Curing them with a fancy light seemed like a neat trick.

I awkwardly gathered up my phone and my baggie, paid, and left a thirty-percent tip. It was the polite thing to do.

I tried to remind myself that I'd accomplished something. But I worried I might have just put myself in even more danger.

I needed to talk to Ben. And to Glenn Swinarski. ASAP.

Chapter Eighteen

IT TOOK me several tries to get my gloves on over those nails as I walked back to the store. Marilyn was right. They were obnoxious. I wondered what I'd have to do to get them off.

Or if I'd survive long enough.

Once inside, I flashed them at Marilyn as I sat down across from her. She'd finished a charity hat and was now working on a mitten in the same yarn. Everything seemed under control in the store. I was still a free agent.

And I was still alive.

"My. Aren't you brave? Did you find out anything good?"

"No," I lied. I didn't like doing it, but I didn't want my dear friend involved. "Now how do I get this stuff off?"

"It's not something you can do at home easily without damaging your natural nails. But they'll probably fall off any minute now. Just wait and see." She snickered at me.

I groaned.

"If not, you can always go back and have someone there take it off."

I groaned again. I didn't fancy going back there anytime soon. Maybe I'd find another salon.

Angie walked by and saw me displaying them. "Whoa. Charlie, did you get your nails done?"

"I did."

"What prompted that?" She picked up my hand and looked at them closely. "So flashy. So unlike you. What are you up to?"

I shrugged. "I felt like a change."

"Mmm," she said doubtfully, and sent me a sideways glance. She wasn't buying it. No one who knew me would.

"I'm going to do some work in my office," I announced before anyone else decided to put in their two cents about my uncharacteristic nail decision.

Comfortably seated in my desk chair, I patted Harvey on the head and pulled out my sock in progress. I needed to think. Knitting would give me something soothing to do and free my mind. The yarn was a new, hand-painted silk-cormo blend made by a famous fiber artisan that would be an exclusive for the store. The pattern I'd chosen was a simple chevron lace to keep the focus on the luxurious yarn, which had both short and long repeats in turquoise, soft yellow, and lime. It occasionally snagged on the dratted nails and I had to hold the needles slightly differently, but nothing was going to stop me. I kept at it until I got a good rhythm going.

The yarn and double-pointed needles went round and round as I thought.

What did I know?

I contemplated the clues I'd gathered.

The dolly that had been left in the Tink Tank had come from the Balser factory where Ben worked. Maybe Ben had borrowed one, or Lauren had filched one at some point in the past, possibly if she'd been at the factory visiting Ben.

I sighed. I didn't know enough about any of that, but I could still ask Ben about it.

The boxes of books could have come from anywhere—an

estate sale, a secondhand store, a library book sale. I didn't think that would be an easy avenue to track down. They weren't notable books in any way. Besides, the police had taken them for evidence. I couldn't explore that avenue even if I wanted to.

The fact that Lauren wore gloves while she worked at the salon was more of a coincidence, I thought. Gloves like that were available in every pharmacy, so widely available anyone could have chosen to use them. But she did have practice being dexterous while wearing them.

The person who'd committed both crimes had some of the pink cotton dishcloth yarn I sold in my store. A lot of people had been on that list of yarn buyers I'd delivered to the police, but I knew that Ben Davies was one of them. He'd bought the yarn for Lauren.

Ben had already been cleared for the Blankenship murder, though the police didn't know that yet. I needed to contact Glenn and give him the thumb drive.

Lauren had lied about the nails she'd had on last week. One of those nails had ended up in Harvey's tail, possibly left in my office during the crime. Innocent people didn't lie about inconsequential things like fingernails. And something that took that much time to create wouldn't be easily forgotten.

Whoever had gotten Mike and Trevor into their respective chairs before tying them up would have to be strong. I'd always assumed that meant the assailant was male, but that wasn't necessarily true. Lauren was tall and thin, but had the toned look of someone who worked out. She might be stronger than she looked.

And angry or frightened people—people feeling strong emotions—could do things that calm people couldn't. Every mother in an emergency situation with young children learned that lesson. I had when twelve-year-old Blaine had broken his arm falling out of a tree. He'd been a big boy, and

I'd carried him to the car and not even thought about it until afterward.

Lauren had slept with Mike Blankenship. Ben and Mike had brawled over it. It had created friction between Ben and Lauren, probably on many levels. They might not even be a couple anymore.

Lauren was likely pregnant. Had Mike Blankenship been the father? Why else would Alice have heard the word paternity at their table while they argued at Libby's? For that matter, it sounded like they hated each other—why would they meet at the diner at all unless they were going to discuss something like that?

Lauren had broken her promise to Ben to stop drinking when she slept with Mike, though I wouldn't have been surprised if Mike had spiked her drink to get that started. He'd been a truly terrible person, and if he hated her, he'd done the whole thing out of spite. I wouldn't put it past him to stoop that low. If that was the case, her anger could be transcendent, because it took consent out of the picture entirely.

Was that enough anger to compel someone to commit murder? Probably.

But...

Had she even been conscious when he'd had sex with her? It was a repulsive thought and brought tears to my eyes. I hoped that wasn't the case, but if it was, she was a victim of rape.

She should have gone to the police instead of becoming a vigilante.

Worse ideas flooded my mind. My knitting fell into my lap unheeded.

Had she gone to the police? And been ignored? I'd heard that happened sometimes, but I liked to think that Abingdon police, especially with the university right there, would be more enlightened. If they had disregarded her claims, had she felt compelled to take matters into her own hands?

I did not like these thoughts. Not at all. My imagination was taking me to sordid places. Worst of all, it seemed like every sordid notion was plausible.

But why was I involved? Why had she tried to kill Trevor? Why use my yarn?

For those questions, I had no answers. All I knew was that Lauren disliked me.

Harvey made a deep harumph and got to his feet. I looked up. Ben Davies stood in the doorway to my office with his knuckles poised to strike the doorframe, a mournful expression on his face.

Chapter Nineteen

I MADE sure my knitting was secure on the needles and set it on my desk as I stood. "We need to talk," I said to Ben. "But not here."

He took a step back as I headed toward him. "Okay. Where?"

I grabbed my purse and glanced into the store. Angie had everything under control. She was helping a yarn customer while two of our college students manned the coffee station. Used to mothering her two elementary-school-aged children, she had excellent management skills. Maybe I should consider making her a shift supervisor and giving her a raise. Then I could take more time off. I waved to her and called, "I'm going upstairs."

She nodded, not bothered by me leaving in the least.

"Upstairs, Harvey," I signaled. It was a break in his routine, but he didn't seem to care. Up the stairs we all tromped.

I paused on the landing of the second floor, my forehead wrinkling in confusion. Gina's door was ajar. That wasn't like her. And she'd said she would be sleeping. I frowned and held up a finger to Ben as I poked my head in the door.

Her apartment was a mess. It was never pristinely tidy like my sister's place, but usually it was organized chaos, with piles of books, notebooks, and art projects cluttering all the available surfaces. Still, I'd never seen her leave her door open, or her floor so cluttered you couldn't walk around easily. Today there were drawers open and items strewn all over the floor in a haphazard manner.

"Gina?" I called. When she didn't answer, I tiptoed down the hallway to her bedroom. The door was open, the bed unmade. No Gina in the bed.

"Is this your apartment?" Ben asked from the doorway. He had a skeptical expression on his face.

"My tenant. My assistant manager, Gina, lives here." I checked the bathroom but it was empty too. She wasn't there. I tried not to panic. Gina was young. She could be unpredictable.

I pulled out my phone and dialed her number. It rang once. Then a robot voice said, "The person you have called is unavailable right now. Press one to leave a message."

That freaked me out. I wasn't sure what it meant. Had she turned her phone off? Was the ringer off? Had she travelled somewhere that didn't have signal?

I pressed one. "Gina, I'm worried about you. You left your apartment open. Call or text me as soon as you get this." Then I texted her too, just as a precaution, hoping she'd see that sooner if her ringer was off.

I took one last look around, closed the door, and plodded up the next flight, my thoughts stuck on what I'd just seen in Gina's apartment—and started leaping to frightening conclusions.

Had Gina's ex—Jacob—snapped? She'd said he was harmless, just annoying. What if she'd underestimated his level of crazy? Gina was such a good judge of character. And she'd dated Jacob for over a year—surely she knew him well enough to know if he was truly a threat. If he was really dangerous she wouldn't have hesitated to go to the police.

I paused on the steps, my heart skipping a beat or two. Or, had Lauren gotten to Gina?

No, no. I urged myself to think it through and not give in to panic. The receptionist had said Lauren was booked all morning except for the nine a.m. slot I'd taken. Lauren knew I knew—and she wouldn't risk not having an alibi before doing something horrible. She was too smart for that. It would be too easy for the police to check if she'd skipped out on an appointment.

I started moving up the stairs again, Ben still following. There had to be a simple explanation for this. Gina must have run a quick errand or gone out to get something to eat. Unless I was wrong all along. Unless the killer was someone else, and they'd come back.

Heart pounding, I turned on my heel and brushed past Ben to return to the landing. I leaned out over the railing until I could see the security panel by the back door. I took in a swift, audible breath. The light was green. The back door was unarmed.

What if someone had come in that way?

The mess in Gina's apartment—it was like someone had been looking for something.

What if the person the murderer had been after on the night they attacked Trevor wasn't me at all—what if it was Gina? Glenn had said they might have targeted me because they thought I knew something. But what if it was Gina who had some incriminating knowledge? Could the murderer have just taken Gina right from under my nose while I went off to get my nails done? Lauren hadn't told me anything. Her reticence could have been her normal snotty behavior and not guilt at all.

Who could the killer be, then? One of Ben's and Mike's

friends? I didn't know any of them, except the three I met briefly at Libby's.

But Gina might have. She was friends with Andrea.

No. No. I was jumping to conclusions with no evidence. These were just some weird coincidences that on a normal day I wouldn't worry about in the slightest. I was succumbing to paranoia after so many terrible things had happened. And I was nervous and scared because I'd just confronted Lauren. It was understandable, but I had to get a grip on myself.

I looked up. Ben stood on the flight above me with his brows raised. Harvey was waiting at the top of the stairs, panting and wagging his tail.

Gina was an adult. She was from a big city and definitely street smart. She was fine. Maybe she was looking for something she'd lost and then went for a walk to clear her head or something. Maybe she ran into someone she knew and was gone longer than she expected. The back door was unarmed because it was the time of day when most of our deliveries came. Gina or Angie had probably disarmed it when UPS came and left it that way, expecting the USPS delivery that was due to come any minute.

I was tempted to go down and arm it again, or go looking through the security video to see what I could find, but I talked myself down.

I needed to stay the course and not get sidetracked. Because if Lauren was the murderer, and it really looked like she was, I'd just thrown some gasoline on her fire. And I needed Ben to help me contain it.

I jogged up to the top of the stairs, unlocked the door to my apartment, and held it open for Harvey and Ben. Ben sat down in my purple overstuffed easy chair, looking uncomfortable. He petted Harvey nervously.

Right. Back to my plan. I had something Ben needed. Gina would call or text me soon with a simple explanation.

I checked my phone to make sure it had a good charge and the ringer was on, and then I settled on the sofa and pulled the thumb drive out of my purse. I began by telling him how I'd obtained it at the Piggly-Wiggly. He instantly looked relieved.

"Thank you for doing that for me. But am I going to get in trouble for what I was doing?"

I bit my lip. "I don't know, Ben. I hope not. I'll put in a good word for you, if it comes down to that, tell them that you're trying to change your life. Maybe if you commit to getting help, Glenn will be easy on you? Right now I think it's more important to remove yourself as a suspect than anything else."

He looked resolved. "I can do that."

I took a deep breath. The rest was harder. "There's more. I have to tell you a few things that will upset you. You need to stay calm and help me find a way to finish this, Ben. I've got some ideas of what we can do, but first—just listen."

He looked so earnest and young. I was about to shatter his world, I thought, and I regretted that. Strong maternal feelings surged in me. I wanted to protect him from this, but he had to know the truth. I didn't know how deep his feelings for Lauren ran. I was about to find out.

He nodded. "I'll do whatever you need. I want this to be over too."

I eyed him. He seemed calm enough. "I know Mike and Lauren slept together."

He winced and his Adam's apple bobbed. He looked sick.

I plowed on. "I also suspect Lauren is pregnant."

He closed his eyes and hung his head, defeated. "She is. The night at the Piggly-Wiggly? I'd just found a pregnancy test in the bathroom trash. I'm pretty sure she knows I saw it. I… just left and didn't go back."

"You could be the father. That could be easily resolved these days. There are tests."

He shook his head. "That's just it, Charlie. I can't be."

I frowned. "Because you used contraceptives? They can fail."

"No. Because I have a… a problem Lauren doesn't know about." He hesitated, looking a bit green, his Adam's apple bobbing repeatedly. "I should have told her a long time ago. It was a mistake to keep it to myself, I guess. I've never told… anyone." The last word came out as an incredulous whisper.

I stayed silent, encouraging him to continue.

"My mom always said if a girl loved me she wouldn't care. I guess I didn't believe her. When I was a kid, my mom refused to have me vaccinated. She has strong feelings about these things. I got the mumps in college and… I'm sterile. It's rare, the doctors say, but I've been tested several times. I couldn't have gotten Lauren pregnant even if I wanted to. There's just nothing there. That baby isn't mine."

Well, that was a bombshell.

He continued, "If there'd been even a chance it was mine, I'd have felt different, I guess. The whole thing got me real upset and that's why I… I went to the Piggly-Wiggly. It was the first drink I'd had in months." He made a small distressed sound. "It was just so hard, knowing she was going to have another man's baby."

"Are you sure Lauren didn't know about your condition?"

"I never told her."

"And you think she knew you saw the pregnancy test in the bathroom?"

He looked embarrassed. "I stormed out and left it on the sink."

That was her motive. She felt rejected because of the pregnancy. The pregnancy Mike had caused.

The back of my tongue tasted metallic. I felt so stressed my body was going haywire. But we were figuring this out, piecing it together, me and my unlikely friend.

"Ben, did Lauren tell you what happened with Mike?"

He looked toward the window that faced the street. "It wasn't easy to hear."

I had misgivings, delving so deep into something so private, but I felt it was important, so I asked, "Did Mike force himself on her?"

His eyes were glossy. "That's what she said. Yeah."

Poor Lauren. Oh, this was so awful in so many ways. I couldn't muster anything to say. A lump was lodged in my throat. Of all the things a man could do to a woman, that was among the most vile. I wanted to hurt him myself. I was glad he couldn't do that ever again to anyone else.

After a moment, Ben went on, still avoiding my gaze, "He was like a brother to me—how could he hurt my girl that way?"

Well, that explained the fight. "I'm so sorry, Ben. Did she go to the police?"

He steepled his hands and touched them to his lips. "No. She said she was afraid to. I think that's because of me. Of all the trouble I've been in. She said they wouldn't believe her."

"Sometimes they don't, but I sure wish she had."

He nodded absently, but then looked at me again, sharply. "Why?"

Poor kid. He had no idea where this was going. I was going to have to navigate this as gently as I could.

"First, I need to ask you a question. Did you have a moving dolly in your possession, at the place you shared with Lauren, that came from Balser?"

His eyebrows came together. "Yeah, I borrowed one when we moved to a new apartment a few months ago. I keep forgetting to take it back."

"I don't think it's at your place anymore, Ben. I think the police have it. As evidence for the attack on Trevor."

He looked shocked. Then realization started to dawn. I

could see him putting it together as his expressions morphed through several versions of realization and dismay.

I told him the rest of what I knew and all the things I suspected. From the yarn to the nail enhancement. The dolly, the books, all of it.

When I finished, he cursed softly. "That doesn't prove she did it. That nail, though…" He winced and looked incredulous. "Do you really think she did it?"

I noticed he wasn't denying it outright. Maybe I was on the right track.

"You know her better than I do. Does she have a vindictive streak? Does she dwell on things people have done to her?"

Ben sighed deeply. "Yes."

"There might be hard evidence. If they lifted prints off of the dolly or any of the other stuff. They've already got mine for comparison. They need hers too."

He looked at me with pleading eyes. "But maybe they'll never solve it. Maybe she can just… get away with it."

I shook my head sadly. "It will never be over until the truth comes out. Do you think you could trust her now, go back to living with her again?"

His face crumpled. "Oh, God. Why would she do this?"

I tried to comfort him by sitting on the chair's arm and embracing him. "She was hurt. She was desperate. It doesn't excuse it, but I can understand it."

He hid his face behind his hands and breathed raggedly.

I kept my voice soft, but it rang with authority, even to my own ears. "Ben. You have to be an adult now. You have to face this. I believe all men need to. I told my boys this and now I'm telling you. You helped create this prison you and Lauren are in right now. Every time you let Mike get away with something that you knew was wrong, he got stronger, more bold. When you didn't speak out, take a stand when he slept with other men's girlfriends or treated women badly, it became normal in his sick, twisted mind. This is rape culture. It grows—not from women not saying no to men—but from *men* not saying no to other *men*. Learn from this. Make sure it never happens again within your circles of male friends. Who we are as people isn't just about what we do when things are black and white—it's about what we do with all the shades of grey that we navigate every single day."

He pulled his hands from his face to look up at me, his mouth gaping slightly, as the realization of his part in this dawned on him.

I let him cry himself out, murmuring and shushing for him.

When he seemed calmer, I said, "Hopefully the prosecutor will be lenient, given what Lauren's been through and the fact that she's pregnant. We can't let this go. We have to give her a chance to confess and let justice be done before she hurts someone else. She's not thinking straight. She tried to kill Trevor and he's done nothing to her. She needs help. This has to end. It's the right thing to do."

"I know. I know. I want to do what's right."

There was one more thing I didn't understand. "Ben, why does Lauren dislike me so much? Why did she involve me in this?"

A strangled laugh coughed from his throat. "She's suspicious of women who are nice to me. I told her you're like an aunt or a mom kinda lady to me, but she never bought it. She's accused me more than once of sleeping with you."

Jealousy, then. Lauren had quite a few issues. I looked down at the young man I'd embraced as warmly as though he were my own son and had to sigh.

"I have an idea of what we can do next, but first I want you to go to the apartment you have with Lauren and confirm that both the yarn and the moving dolly are gone. We need to be sure about that before we move forward. But I think we should do it as soon as possible. I got her all worked up this morning at the salon." And Gina still hadn't texted me back, I realized. "We don't want to give her a chance to make things worse or hurt anyone else."

He swallowed convulsively but was starting to look a little calmer. "Okay. I'll call in sick and go check right now."

Chapter Twenty

I GOT A TEXT FROM BEN. *You were right. Neither thing is here. Coming back.*

I texted back, *Okay*. Though it was ten times harder to use my phone with those blasted nails on my fingers. I still hadn't heard from Gina yet, though I'd left another message. Or two. I had to talk myself down from calling the police every few minutes. But now I had stuff to do to keep me busy.

With Ben's confirmation, I could proceed.

Maybe I was foolish, but I thought I could handle this better than the police would.

I made an action list. It sat on my desk and I began to check things off as I did them.

First, I printed out two signs for the restrooms: *Out of Order.* I confirmed that the rooms were empty, put the signs in place, and locked the bathroom doors from the outside. Coffee tended to make things expedient, and that would begin to clear out the store. Check.

I told my employees to inform customers of our plumbing difficulties when they made purchases. Check.

In a half hour, I'd politely tell anyone who was left that I was having to close the store for the afternoon due to plumbing problems.

I brought Angie into my office. I didn't tell her anything she didn't need to know. I asked her if she knew who Ben Davies and Lauren Waters were. She said she did. I told her that as soon as Ben and Lauren were served, Angie was to get any remaining customers—aside from Ben and Lauren—out of the store as quietly as possible, lock the front door, flip the open sign to closed, and she as well as the rest of the baristas were to leave silently through the back. They'd be paid for their normal shift and I'd call them if we reopened later. I asked her to remind everyone that they weren't to gossip in the store, no matter how tempting. She raised her brows, but agreed. Plenty of weird things had happened in our shop lately. I guess to her this seemed minor by comparison. Check.

Then I called Glenn Swinarski. My nerves got jangly when it took him forever to pick up, but he did eventually.

I didn't tell him much except that I had found some evidence in my store I needed him to see. I asked if he would consider freeing up his afternoon to come talk to me about it. I told him it might take a little while and that I felt it was really urgent. I'd explain when he got there. And could he please park around back so my customers wouldn't get worried? Keeping him in the dark for now made more sense than arguing with him over the phone. He agreed to come. He was clearly curious, and he needed a break in the case at any rate. Thankfully he didn't even bring up my adventure at Balser the day before. Check.

Ben returned. I briefly explained my plan, and he agreed it was a kinder way to proceed. We decided it would be best to wait until we'd talked to Glenn together, and then he'd walk down to Phalanges and return with Lauren.

"Why don't you call her now and tell her you miss her or something like that?" I asked. "If you've been avoiding each other, showing up at the salon might result in a fight instead of what we want. It might be best to soften things, make her receptive to talking."

I offered to leave him alone to call her in my office or upstairs, but he asked me to stay. "I need the moral support," he said. So I remained nearby.

I only heard one side of the conversation, but he did well. He told her he wanted to talk, and she must have agreed because he said he'd be over in a little while.

He lowered his cell phone and said, "She says she's not feeling well today. She's lying down in the break room right now. She said she was booked all morning, but doesn't have anything scheduled for the afternoon."

Check.

When Glenn came in, Angie's eyes grew wide as saucers. I ushered Glenn upstairs to my apartment. Ben was ashen and silent as he eased back into the purple chair. Glenn sat down on the lime green one as I explained about the moving dolly and the fact that Lauren had lied about the nails. Then the pregnancy and Mike's involvement. And Ben's alibi and how his reaction to the pregnancy test on the night of the murder might have set Lauren in motion.

Glenn brushed his thumb and forefinger down his steel-grey mustache. "There's means, motive, and opportunity, right there. Is she working in the salon? I'll have to take her in for questioning."

Ben looked even paler. "Yes, but—" He turned his gaze on me, silently imploring.

I spoke up. "Glenn, I was hoping you'd consider a different, softer approach, given the sensitive nature of what we're dealing with."

He looked at me sternly. "If she committed these crimes—"

I nodded. "She may be guilty, but she's also a victim. And

she's pregnant. I think Ben and I can get her to confess, easier than a bunch of scary men in uniforms will. Won't that make things easier for her and for you?"

He eyed me. I could tell he was wavering.

"Please, Glenn. I know it's not normal procedure. But we can do this. All that really matters is solving the crime, right?"

He frowned. "Charlotte Shaw, you are a big-hearted woman."

I explained my plan and that it was already in process. He reluctantly agreed. We continued to work through my checklist. Ben went off to Phalanges to get Lauren. Glenn was set up in my office with a coffee, to watch the CCTV footage live and listen with the door open.

The store had already emptied, so Angie and I took off our aprons and sat off to one side at a table that hadn't been cleared yet, to look like customers. I kept checking my phone for messages from Gina, but she was still silent. I hoped I was right. About her. And about Lauren.

Ethan, my EIU student from Australia, brought us a couple of lattes and bussed the table. "This is all very cloak and dagger, innit?" he said with a grin. "Very clever. Very clever, indeed. No one wanted to stick around when we said the toilet was out of order."

I was feeling a bit on edge, but I managed a slight smile. "Just play your part, Ethan."

"No worries." He good-naturedly wiped off the table and went back to the coffee counter.

I tried not to stare obviously out the window, but when I saw Ben running across the street, alone, I stood up and gaped at him.

He came in, breathless. "She's not there. They said she just left a minute ago and didn't say where she was going."

Chapter Twenty-One

GLENN EMERGED from my office and let out a florid curse.

I flinched.

My plan had fallen apart and I looked like a fool.

"Where would she go?" I asked Ben. "We have to find her."

I felt all the blood drain from my head and sat down in the nearest chair. "What if she has Gina?"

Angie and Ethan looked confused and horrified.

"What?" Glenn said. His face had gone scarlet.

I stuttered, "Gina lives upstairs in one of the apartments. I found her door open an hour ago or so, and her place looked like it had been ransacked. I thought… "

"And you didn't think that was important enough to tell me?" Glenn stormed. This was the first time I'd ever seen the man angry, and it was intimidating. "This is why you should leave the detective work to the police, Ms. Shaw. You've withheld several key pieces of evidence in the last twenty-four hours. You've made a complete mess of this investigation and now we may have a murderer loose in town—with a hostage."

He didn't give me a chance to explain. He turned away

and spoke into the radio on his shoulder. "Dispatch, send Jones and Ramirez my way. I need extra hands. Take down this description of a person of interest in the Blankenship murder..." He rattled off a thorough description of Lauren and barked further instructions. He swung back around to face me. "Show me Gina's apartment."

I hustled upstairs and opened her door for him with Ben trailing behind.

Glenn took a brief look around then got on the phone. He hovered a discreet distance from me and gave me the stink eye while he spoke. I shifted uncomfortably from foot to foot, feeling miserable because of how badly I'd failed.

And Gina might be paying for my mistakes.

More police arrived. They combed over Gina's possessions, taking photos and bagging and tagging some of her things. While the other officers were doing that, Glenn interviewed Ben at length in my office. I stood in the middle of Gina's living room, mute and nauseated with fear for Gina, afraid to touch anything or say anything. Since it was my property, I had to be there, but there was nothing I could do. I felt helpless.

When they finished, Glenn had some parting words for me. "You stay put. I'm still deciding if I should file charges for obstruction of justice."

Then he swept out, and I was left standing on the landing outside Gina's apartment. I felt dazed. How had this gone so monumentally wrong? I didn't know, but I needed time to think.

Angie appeared at the bottom of the stairs, looking uncharacteristically shy. "Should I reopen the shop?"

"No, send everyone home and take the day."

Angie nodded and I remained where I was, lost in thought, as my employees gathered their jackets and left through the back door. Ben stood next to me, absorbed in his phone.

He seemed to feel my eyes on him and looked up. "I'm texting friends to see if they've seen her."

I heard a faint whine from upstairs and moved numbly toward my apartment. Harvey had heard all the commotion and was unsettled because he couldn't see me. "I'll make some tea," I said.

Harvey snuffled me all over as I entered, and then stayed glued to my side as I set a kettle on the stove and spooned loose-leaf tea into an infusing basket. I didn't know Lauren well enough to be able to predict what she'd do next.

Had something Ben said to Lauren tipped her off? Or had it been my visit to the salon that spooked her? Would she hurt Gina? Or had she taken her hostage to use as a human shield to get out of town? And why Gina?

Maybe she was the easiest target close to me. She wanted to shut me up.

And I hadn't taken the hint. Bringing the police in had probably just put Gina in even more danger.

I forced myself to think it all through, logically. I saw Gina before I went to Phalanges. Lauren had not been punctual right at 9:00 a.m., but how could Lauren have kidnapped Gina, stashed her somewhere, and gotten to Phalanges so fast? Could she have grabbed Gina, stuffed her in her trunk, and driven straight to work? That was possible, I supposed, but I doubted that Gina would go unnoticed in a car trunk in a parking lot downtown all this time. On the other hand, if she'd hurt her badly... or worse...

My body was clenched up tight. Every muscle ached from the tension. I'd been so foolish.

The water boiled and I poured it over the tea leaves with shaky hands. I could hear the little sounds Ben's phone made as he typed, sending and receiving texts from where he sat on the sofa in the next room.

Would this ever be over? Would the police catch her and

rescue Gina? Or would Lauren kill Gina and run, leaving me with all this guilt and a shadow of fear hanging over my shoulder for the rest of my life? Could my sons be in danger too?

I had to sit down. I left the tea steeping on the counter and moved to sit down on a chair in the living room. Harvey put his head on my knee, his big brown eyes full of worry. I patted him absently and picked up the knitting project sitting on the side table. I began to knit without even thinking about it as I, again, thought through the details.

One suddenly jumped out at me. I'd forgotten in the tempest of emotions. The security cameras had probably picked up Lauren and Gina. I could at least let Glenn know what time she had been there, how she was treating Gina, and, if I was lucky, the direction she'd left in. That might give the police something to work with. If Glenn hadn't been so mad at me, he probably would have looked at that before he left. But maybe he wanted to get the manhunt started first and he'd be back later.

I mumbled something about it to Ben and stood, setting my knitting aside and picking up my phone. I'd taken two steps toward the door when it slammed open.

Lauren stood there. She looked incensed. "I knew it. Look at you two here all cozy. I don't know why you ever denied it."

Harvey got to his feet and let out a low growl.

"Harvey, down," I commanded. I put a finger to my lips to tell him to stay silent and prayed he'd obey me. He huffed and got down to the floor, but he didn't relax. His head stayed raised and alert, watching Lauren.

I watched her too. Her chest was heaving as her contemp-tuous gaze lingered on Harvey. I feared for a moment that she might try to hurt him. Then she swung back to Ben, still sitting on the sofa. "What do you have to say for yourself? You were cheating on me with her the whole time, weren't you?"

Ben seemed accustomed to her volatile moods—he wasn't surprised or afraid in any way, despite what I'd told him. His reaction was to roll his eyes as if he'd heard this a million times. "Come on, Lauren. I've been texting you, trying to find you."

Her lip curled in disdain. "I know. You've been here all day. I've been tracking your phone. Imagine my surprise when you call me from here, acting all sweet like you want to get back together—but you've been in bed with this old bag the whole time. And then the police were here." She refocused on me. "What did you tell them?"

"You're tracking my phone?" Ben sounded exasperated. He shook his head in disbelief.

My heart thumped in my chest like I was a frightened rabbit, a fresh surge of adrenaline coursing through my tired body. I licked my lips to speak, but Ben stood, reaching for Lauren's hand before I could say anything.

"Sit down, Lauren. We're on your side," Ben said firmly, already recovered from the shock of Lauren's invasion of his privacy. He grabbed her hand and pulled her toward my couch.

Lauren resisted the pull and held her ground. "Not her. She's not," Lauren accused, glaring at me. "What did she tell you? Some lies about me?"

I glared back. "Where's Gina, Lauren?"

Lauren's pretty face contorted with contempt. "How should I know?"

Ben was still holding Lauren's hand. He glanced at me for reassurance, then looked up into Lauren's face with an earnest, sad expression. "There are some things I need to say to you, things I wasn't smart enough to realize on my own, but I'm an idiot and they're true. First, I—I'm so sorry. I'm ashamed to say that it's partly my fault Mike was such a monster, that he hurt you. I should have stood up to him, a long time ago, when we were kids. I never should have stood by when he did terrible things to people—to women, especially. I let him off the hook too many times. That was wrong." He finished with glassy downcast eyes, then looked back up at her. "I hope someday you can forgive me for that."

She looked surprised and confused. She finally allowed herself to be pulled down next to Ben on the sofa. I noted where her purse landed and where she kept her hands. Could she have done the awful things I thought she had? Why had she come here? What was her plan? Did she have a weapon?

I felt like anything could happen, but the tension had subsided a little. I backed into the lime-colored chair and eased down cautiously, still holding my silent phone.

Lauren reached out to caress Ben's hair, like a curious child, like she'd forgotten I was there. She looked exhausted, small and delicate.

"Mike was a bad man," I said, leaning forward. "I'm sorry he assaulted you. But I wish you'd gone to the police instead of taking justice into your own hands."

"Oh, shut up," she directed at me then turned her gaze back on Ben. Her expression softened toward him, her eyes searching his face.

Ben looked beaten down. His Adam's apple bobbed. "I know what you did with the Balser dolly. And the pink yarn I gave you for your birthday."

She stuttered, leaning away from him. "That... It..."

I felt the need to press her further. I decided to bluff, but kept my voice gentle since she seemed to be faltering, on the verge of confession. I hoped. "One of your nails fell off in my office while you were here that morning with Trevor Fontenay. The police took it as evidence and submitted it to a forensics lab. They'll get your DNA from it. It's only a matter of time."

"No!" she cried. Her voice rang with a tinge of mania. "No! It's not supposed to be like this. Come on, Ben. This baby is yours. I know it in my heart. Let's just go somewhere where we can live in peace and raise him together. It will be so easy."

"The baby isn't mine," Ben said, his voice echoing with regret.

"Yes it is! Let's just start over somewhere new!"

He told her how he knew the baby wasn't his.

Tears streamed down her face. She kept shaking her head no. "All I ever wanted was to be safe. With you. I—I just... I've been so scared. You have to believe me, Ben. I just did what I had to do to be safe..."

All the energy seemed to have gone out of her. She looked like a broken porcelain doll. We were so close to getting her to confess. If we could do that, the rest should fall into place, shouldn't it? I was still contemplating this when I caught movement in my peripheral vision.

Glenn stood behind the partially open door, just out of Lauren's view. I tried not to stare. If Lauren saw me looking over there, it would tip her off and we'd never get the confession out of her.

Glenn was gesturing at me like a baseball coach. I had no idea what he was trying to say. I glanced at Lauren to make sure she was still gazing at Ben like she was moonstruck and flashed Glenn a warning look, hoping he would understand that I was telling him to stay where he was and be quiet. It worked. He stopped trying to signal to me and braced himself against the doorframe to listen.

"Just tell us the truth," Ben said. "Don't you think it'll be easier for you than if they catch you with the evidence?"

"But they—I'm not even a suspect," she mumbled. She slumped, the arrogant posture and attitude completely gone. She seemed to be caving in on herself, getting smaller.

"They know everything, Lauren," Ben said calmly.

I was proud of him for staying strong. And so glad Glenn was close in case things went south.

"I thought you loved me," she whispered.

Ben closed his eyes, his expression a rictus of anguish. "That's why I want you to tell us the truth."

Her mouth twisted, turning here face into an ugly facsimile of itself, her anger rising again, her body inflating slightly. "So I can go to jail and you can be with your precious Charlotte?"

"No, Lauren. You know Ben and I are just friends," I said.

Her lower lip quivered. "Do you really think they'd go easier on me?"

She was asking me. Sincerely. I didn't know what to make of that. But I answered honestly. "I do, Lauren. I want you to have every chance at a fair trial. I'll help you if I can."

She stared at us in turn, searching for something in our expressions. She must have found it. "I'm so tired. I can't... I killed Mike Blankenship because he raped me and probably tons of other women and I didn't want him to hurt me or anyone else anymore."

A moment of peace settled over me. Relief. It was over.

But that was short-lived. "Where's Gina?" I prodded urgently, trying not to break the current mood, but scared to death for my friend.

Lauren rolled her eyes in my direction, a hint of her normal self rising back up. "Why do you keep asking me about her? I don't know where she is."

I frowned and tried another angle. "Why did you attack Trevor Fontenay? My security guard?"

Lauren shrugged and clung to Ben possessively, her voice muffled and choked. "I used the yarn on Mike because I thought they might arrest you, but they didn't. I wanted you to stop flirting with Ben. I know he likes you. And that hurts. So much. I... was angry. I wanted to hurt you back. But it was stupid. It wasn't the same thing as Mike. I realized that and I —it probably doesn't matter, but I changed my mind and tried to cut him free. I just suddenly knew it was a mistake. But I was so scared to get caught—I had to leave before I could finish. Oh, God, I'm glad Trevor didn't die. He—he never hurt me."

Her voice was so small, like a child's at the end. Maybe it was an affectation or maybe it was just all the hurt pushing through. It didn't matter. What was clear to me was that she needed help—and she'd never learned how to be vulnerable enough to ask for it. She had learned to brazen her way through life, while inside, she crumbled.

Glenn chose that moment to let his presence be known. He pushed the door open the rest of the way and stood there silently. Lauren didn't even look surprised. She sighed and hid her face against Ben's chest.

It was over. We'd gotten the confession. Glenn would take her into custody and things would return to normal.

Except—where was Gina? Lauren had been shockingly honest about everything. I felt sure that if she'd taken Gina, she would have admitted it. So, where was my friend?

My phone pinged over and over in rapid succession. I looked down. It was a series of texts from Gina that seemed to arrive all at once.

Sorry. My phone died. I'm nearly dead myself. So tired.

Got called to campus for those political shenanigans I mentioned. They weren't actually over. They're still not over.

I left my apartment in a hurry. Have you seen my bus pass? I can't find it anywhere.

Be back soon to collapse. How are things there?

Gina was just fine and had never been in any danger. I sunk back into the chair with the additional relief. Then I told Glenn.

All his attention was on Lauren, but he nodded and glanced at me with chagrin. "Good. I'm glad I came back to apologize for being so rough on you."

I sighed. "You weren't wrong. I did make a mess of things."

His mustache twitched. "That you did. But I should have been more diplomatic about it."

Glenn was kind. He didn't put cuffs on Lauren. He just read her rights and led her out to his car through the back. She didn't fight it. I thought she might be in shock. I hoped the baby would be okay.

Ben and I stood together in the alley, Harvey between us, as they drove away.

Chapter Twenty-Two

I LOOKED AROUND THE SHOP. Everything seemed to be in place. "Are we ready to unlock the doors?" I called out to the crowd in general.

Nods and smiles and cheers of "Yes!" answered me.

I tried to shake off the pall hanging over me from attending Lauren Waters's arraignment the day before. There was no reason not to enjoy this cheerful occasion. We'd been advertising that we were having a grand opening of our first art installation today, and we'd just been closed for two hours over lunch to prepare.

Regular coffees would be free for the next few hours, and Vincent had volunteered to provide cupcakes. He stood by them now, admiring his own work on a central table where he'd set up a display of multiple layers of beautifully decorated tiny cakes that made my mouth water. He tweaked one here and there so it sat just so.

Andrea beamed. Her colorful artwork in watercolors and oils was displayed expertly all around the shop. We'd worked together to make sure they were hung just as professionally as they would be in any gallery. It was easy to see that she was proud of her work. And pride was justified. When I'd first thought of displaying her art, I'd assumed it would be the tattoo examples she had hanging up next door.

I should have known there was more to it than that. That there was more to her.

She did amazing portraits of people, both real and imagined, in a style that reflected both skill at rendering the human form, and a use of color that took my breath away. Some of the people she'd depicted so realistically might be considered ugly by mainstream American culture, the way she used color to give them expression and depth made them beautiful. There was even one of me in muted greys, silver, and blues with red accents. She'd made my eyes look like they were made of galaxies and my lips a mixture of bold reds that made me think of a heart. Though my hair was hanging in waves around my shoulders and not in its tidy braid, and I never saw my lips reflected in the mirror looking like that, she'd captured the essence of me somehow.

We were ready. I flipped my key in the lock and turned the sign in the window. Then I blocked the door open to let in the fresh spring air.

We didn't have to wait long. The warm weather had lured people outside to walk the downtown streets in droves, and even people who didn't know about the art installation were stopping to see what was going on in my shop. The balloons and streamers I'd hung outside had been a good investment.

I worked the room, making sure to have a conversation with everyone who came in, upselling everyone's contributions shamelessly with a smile on my face. I watched Andrea as she shyly answered questions about her work. It was good that the spotlight was on her now, after all these years of feeling like she was in her brother's shadow. Now her light could shine.

Ben came up to me, a coffee in one hand and a cupcake in the other.

"How are you doing?" I asked him, my smile fading.

"Okay," he said. "Thanks for your help with the lawyer. He seems smart."

"It was mostly my sister, Becca," I replied. "She knows everyone."

"I never knew Andrea did all this," he said, his eyes roving around the room.

I nodded. "I don't think anyone did. She kept it to herself. Her private joy."

"Sometimes you have to look a little harder at people to notice how special they are," he said. Then he took a bite of his cupcake and wandered off to look at the artwork more closely.

Truer words were rarely spoken by someone so young.

Heartbreak was a ruthless teacher.

I saw Glenn Swinarski over in a corner and walked over to say hello.

"It's nice to be here under more pleasant circumstances," he said. It looked like maybe a smile had emerged under his enormous mustache.

"I agree wholeheartedly."

"No more sleuthing for you, young lady. You keep your focus on stuff like this. You're good at it. Leave the investigations to me."

"Happily!" I exclaimed.

He tilted his head, and I saw his lower lip working under that mustache. "Maybe you and I could find other pleasant circumstances to share sometime. Together."

I blinked. Then I blurted out, "Glenn Swinarski, are you asking me out on a date?"

"Maybe. Are you going to say yes?"

My mouth opened for a few moments in sheer surprise. My gut instinct was to let him down easy, but Marci's advice—that I deserved a comforting companion—had stuck in my thoughts. I wavered, suddenly realizing I was unsure. I'd been focused on my store for so long that a lot of my old friendships had withered. Maybe it was time to start a new kind of life. The whole thought process probably played out on my face, plain for him to see. "I don't know. I'll have to think about it."

His lower lip disappeared, and his bushy brows came down, his eyes earnest. "There's no pressure and no hurry on my part."

I summoned a rueful smile. "It's... complicated. Can we talk about this later? I want to explain my thoughts when I'm not in such a jumble. There's too much going on right now. But my answer is maybe. How's that?"

"My timing's not always the best. My apologies. I'll respect whatever answer you give me."

I squeezed his arm. "Don't worry about it. We'll talk. Okay? Excuse me, my sister is calling my name."

He chuckled. "So I hear."

Everyone could hear. Everyone was looking at Rebecca. I made my way over to her immediately so she'd quiet down.

"Charlotte, why don't you sell these cupcakes here in your shop?" she accused. "They are *divine*."

Becca had returned home after Lauren was arrested and indicted, which had happened very quickly. The whole county was relieved that the mysterious murder had finally been solved. I was additionally relieved to have my apartment back —all to myself. And Harvey.

And to get a decent night of sleep.

I turned to Vincent, who was standing right next to her. "I don't know. Why don't I sell these cupcakes in the Tink Tank?"

"I don't know. I didn't know you wanted cupcakes," he said.

"I didn't know I wanted them either."

We laughed.

Like I'd hoped, Vincent had gotten friendlier now that I

knew his secret, instead of shying away. It was a relief that my nosiness hadn't ruined a good friendship. In the last couple of weeks we'd even done a few things together, like jointly sourcing supplies and ingredients to save money by buying in bulk. I'd met his partner, who commuted to Cedar Rapids for work. And Becca and Gina and I had even gone out to dinner with them once. It was nice.

Andrea came up behind me and grabbed my arm. "I've sold three paintings already, Charlotte! I could kiss you! Thank you!"

I tapped my cheek. "Put it right there, like the French do."

"Oui, oui!" she cried, giving me dramatic kisses on both cheeks, and then she flitted off on a bubble, so happy she looked like a different person from the morose young woman who used to slink around in the alley, smoking.

Andrea didn't know it yet, but I'd just bought her building a few days before. Her landlord was aging and letting it go for a song. He'd come to me directly this time, and offered it to me for even less than the last time I'd inquired. He just didn't want to deal with it anymore. I figured owning it myself would be safer in the long run for both me and Andrea than waiting to see who bought it. It would keep my options open for the future, in case she decided to relocate her business.

I'd already decided to keep her rent the same, but to fix up the infrastructure, which I assumed had been neglected all these years. And I'd modestly remodel the apartments upstairs for additional income as my budget allowed.

Gina went by with one of our huge coffee urns. I followed, to help her get it up in its spot. They were heavy. I checked over our stock of everything. She'd been keeping on top of it well.

"We're going through this fast, but we're also selling a lot of espresso drinks," she whispered.

I beamed. "Good. Looks like it's a win-win for everyone."

It was indeed.

———

EVERY TIME A READER leaves a review an author gets her wings... and dozens of new readers find their next new adventure. If you enjoyed this Jessa Archer mystery, would you please take just a moment to let others know?

More Cozies from Jessa Archer

Canterbury Golf Club Mysteries
The Mystery of the Missing Crystal Golf Ball (Free Mini
Mystery)
A Murder at the Country Club
A Murder at the Devil's Ball

Legal Beagle Cozy Mysteries
Hound on the Sound (Free Mini Mystery)
Scales of Justice
Treble with the Law

About the Author

Jessa Archer writes sweet, funny, warm-hearted cozy mysteries because she loves a good puzzle and can't stand the sight of blood. Her characters are witty, adventurous, and crafty in the nicest way. You'll find her sleuths hand lettering inspirational quotes, trying to lower golf handicaps, enjoying a scone at a favorite teashop, knitting a sweater, or showing off a dramatic side in local theater.

Jessa's done many things in her long career, including a stint as a journalist and practicing law. But her favorite job is spinning mysteries. She loves playing small-town sleuth and transporting readers to a world where the scones are delicious, wine pairs with hand lettering, and justice always prevails.

If you want to know when Jessa's next book will be available, visit her website, www.jessaarcher.com where you can sign up for her newsletter.

Printed in Great Britain
by Amazon

16359115R00130